You Can Come
HOME AGAIN

Michelle Cuce

ISBN 978-1-63784-001-6 (paperback)
ISBN 978-1-63784-006-1 (digital)

Cover by Amy Brancato

Hawes & Jenkins Publishing
16427 N. Scottsdale Road, Suite 410
Scottsdale, AZ 85254

Printed in the United States of America

*This book is dedicated to anyone who
believes in the power of love.*

Hunter looked out the window of the black town car he was seated in the back of, the grey, gloomy weather overwhelming him with an annoyance that prickled under his skin. For November, this was very typical weather in Peggy's Cove, but Hunter was used to New York, where it was still crisp, autumn weather. The cold bothered Hunter, and even in the warmth of the car, he pulled his wool pea coat tighter. They pulled up to the two level home nearly forty minutes after departing the airport. The lower level of the house was covered in grey wood shingles, while the upper level boasted slate blue wood shingles. White framed windows flanked with weathered raspberry shutters were scattered among both levels of the house. Hunter tipped and thanked the driver, pulled his bags from the trunk, and let himself into the empty home. He knew the place would be empty, his parents at a doctor's appointment, his sister at their restaurant. He slowly trudged through the house he grew up in, a cold chill slithering down his spine, the rustic decor making him physically ill. Five years away from this place had not been long enough. Sure, he missed his family, but they had been kind enough to visit him when they could and keep in touch electronically. He adamantly refused to return to Peggy's Cove, that is until now. His father had taken a fall on black ice and needed time to recover before returning to work. His mom had asked him to help, then his sister told him it wasn't a question when he had said no. Hunter kicked off his shoes in the small entryway, walked past the living room and up the back staircase to his old room, left completely intact. He dropped his duffle bag on the bed and dragged his suitcases against the wall under his window. He ran his hand over the top of the dresser, checking for dust, and was surprised to find it had been newly cleaned. He dug a beanie out of his duffle, pulled it on snugly over his thick black hair and turned on his heel to head back out the door. Ten minutes was enough that he needed air and why not reacquaint himself with the town? Six months, his mom had said that his father would be back to work in six months. Hunter pulled the door closed and locked it with the key he remembered to grab from his apartment before flying back to Peggy's Cove. He pulled up the collar of his calf length black pea coat so it stood up around his neck and tightened his matching black cashmere scarf to keep warm. He walked down toward the main road running through a mental list of his clients and accounts he had been working on. He was sure he had crossed every t and dotted every i more than once, but he was meticulous and he wanted to be absolutely sure everything was in order back home in New York. He found himself turning left at the lighthouse and walking toward the wharf as he rattled off a list of vendors he had contacted, mumbling to himself. His focus was abruptly pulled away when he crashed into a short woman with dark wavy hair. The crunch of boxes and crates filled the air as the heavy load she was carrying fell to the ground.

"Shit, watch where you're going!" Hunter grumbled, his eyebrows knit together in frustration as he brushed dirt from the front of his pea coat.

"Oh my gosh, I'm so sorry! I just didn't see you there and…" the girl spoke at the same time as him, tripping over her apology and looked up at him as she tucked her long espresso waves behind her ear, "Hunter?" Her deep chestnut eyes widened in surprise.

"Wait Shay?" He squinted at her, recognizing her quickly.

"Oh my gosh!" Shay smiled brightly, wrapping him in a warm hug and he brought his arms around her.

"I can't believe you're here." She said, pulling back from him.

"It's so good to see you!" He smiled and was met with a smack to his bicep that hurt more than it should have from someone her size. "Ouch what the fuck?"

"That's for dropping off the face of the Earth." Shay lost her smile, looking at the ground between them as Hunter rubbed his arm where she'd hit him, "I called you. I texted you. I left you so many messages. You never returned any of them." Her voice became quiet, something that surprised Hunter. Shay was sarcastic, sassy, brutally honest, at least, five years ago she was.

"I didn't think it would matter." He narrowed his eyes skeptically.

Shay scoffed, raking her fingers through her hair and shrugged, "Of course it mattered. You were my friend, like my only...friend." She mumbled so quietly, Hunter almost missed it. He shook his head, an attempt to clear his mind and clarify what he had just heard.

"I...you...we were-ARE. Ugh Shay. I...didn't." He stumbled over his words running his hands down his face, stress evident on his face and Shay smirked at him.

"I forgive you, but you owe me a pizza." She pointed at him and his shoulders visibly relaxed.

"I can do that." Hunter nodded vigorously.

"Also beer. Lots of beer." She said and he sighed, "Yea, I can do that too." Hunter gave her a half smile, only the left side of his mouth turning up, "Meet me at the pizza window, eight o'clock?"

"You got it." She nodded picking up the box and crate, she stacked one on top of the other. "Bye!" She yelled back as she walked away. Hunter shook his head and turned to walk back to his parents' house.

"His bags are upstairs; I checked when we got back. He probably went to check the restaurant, my sweet boy." Beth smiled, busying herself in the kitchen. She was talking a mile a minute, eager for Hunter to return to the house. She picked up a framed picture of their family and sighed. It was from their town Christmas party the year before Hunter moved to New York. She was noticeably younger, her skin smoother, hair bouncier. She was comfortably nuzzled in her husband's arms, Hunter and Katie on either side of them, three big smiles, one coy smirk. Beth held the frame close to her chest as the key clicked into the lock.

"He's home!" She smiled brightly placing the picture back on the mantle and scurried back to the kitchen just as Hunter entered the room, coat still on. "My baby!" She hugged him tightly.

"Hi Mom." Hunter rolled his eyes wrapping his arms around her small frame. The top of her head just barely met his shoulder. He noticed she felt thinner than the last time he had seen her, then couldn't remember when that was. Six months ago? Eight months?

"Honey, thank you so much for being here, for helping out. It means so much to us; really you're rescuing our family."

"It's fine Mom." He shrugged her off and she held his arms taking a step back.

"I want to look at you! My boy." She smiled brightly, "You look great sweetie." She said cupping his cheek just before he ducked away.

"There he is! So glad to have you here son." Jack smiled as Katie pushed his wheelchair into the kitchen. His leg was propped up on a cushion, extended straight out in front of him, parallel to the ground, arm pulled across his body in a sling.

"I'm making lasagna tonight! Everyone's favorite family dinner!" Beth smiled beginning to gather ingredients.

"Oh I'm meeting Shay for pizza tonight. I figured everyone had eaten." Hunter said. Beth's smile faltered, but just for a moment.

"That's okay honey, we can have lasagna tomorrow night! I should have told you it's my fault."

"Thanks Mom, tomorrow's great." Hunter nodded and grabbed a water bottle before heading up to his room. He hung his coat neatly and fixed the beanie on his head before he resituated the scarf around his neck, careful not to crease it. Katie let herself in and slammed the door behind her, loud enough to make Hunter jump and spin to face her.

"What do you want Katie." He huffed as a statement more than a question.

"You have some nerve you know?" She yanked the scarf from around his neck letting it hang from her hand sweeping the floor.

"What the fuck? That scarf is more exp—"

5

"Good then I have your attention." She narrowed her eyes as Hunter groaned aloud his hands clenching two fists at his sides, but he did not speak. "Mom has been talking about you coming home like it's her job. From the moment you said yes, she has been planning this stupid lasagna dinner because it's your favorite. She spent all day yesterday shopping and dusting this room, as if she doesn't already do it regularly, and for what? An ungrateful son to waltz in and out without so much as a hello and leave to have dinner with his long lost friend that he hasn't spoken to in years." Katie was mad. Wasn't she always mad though? Everything seemed to piss Katie off all the time. Hunter watched her, his own anger heating up inside his chest, as she waved her arms wildly, her perfect chestnut curls bouncing against her pink cheeks, flushed with agitation.

"I'm not here to play house Katie."

"You had better be here for dinner tomorrow or I swear I—"

"Fine, yes I'll be here. Now give me my scarf and leave me alone." He seethed through clenched teeth. She dropped the scarf to her feet and flicked her hair as she left the room.

Hunter arrived at the pizza window five minutes early with two six packs in tow. When Shay met him, he ordered them a pizza and they found a bench on the dimly lit dock to sit, pizza box and beers between them.

"I'm surprised my parents didn't tell you I was coming." Hunter said before he took his first bite.

"Katie mentioned you may come, but they didn't want anyone to know in case you didn't show." She shrugged, sipping her beer.

"Well here I am." He smirked coyly and she rolled her eyes at him.

"So what do you do in New York? Must be so busy and important that you couldn't *ever* come back to Peggy's Cove." she said, the sarcasm he was so familiar with returning to her voice.

"I'm in events. I plan events at a museum. I also work privately with artists to plan shows to display and sell their work. " He preened, his chest puffing out slightly.

"Wow, okay I guess that is impressive." Shay smirked and Hunter smiled proudly, "So you actually live in the city?" She asked curiously.

"Not when I first moved there. I lived in Brooklyn with three roommates, which was…interesting? But I make a substantial commission on each piece I curate, so once that started coming in I moved to lower Manhattan and got an apartment of my own."

"Hmm that explains the fancy cape." Shay's shark like grin spread on her face as she nodded her chin in his direction.

"This is a coat. A wool pea coat made specifically for excessively cold temperatures." He defended picking up another slice.

"Mmhmm your chattering teeth say it's doing a fantastic job." Shay rolled her eyes sarcastically, finishing off her beer. It was then that he noticed she was only wearing a hoodie and jeans, seemingly unbothered by what he could only describe as frigid temperatures.

"So what kept you here? What do you do?" Hunter asked his face scrunching in detest for the small town.

"My family owns Lighthouse Lane Cottages. When my parents moved to mainland Canada I took it over." She shrugged nonchalantly.

"Your family must be doing well for themselves." He nodded going for a third slice and popping open another beer.

"I send my parents a cut monthly and the rest goes back to the town." Shay shrugged.

"You've gone soft." He eyed her skeptically.

"Instead of accusing me, why don't you just ask me why?" She was met with raised eyebrows promoting her to go on. She sighed heavily, "Two years ago, just a few months after my parents left, there was a storm. It came out of nowhere. There wasn't a cloud in the sky, until there was. Everything changed. We lost fifteen fishermen that day."

"That's like—"

"Half the town? Yea," Shay laughed humorlessly, "not one survivor." She shook her head.

"I-I didn't know." He said quietly.

"And what would you have done if you did?" She challenged him. He opened and closed his mouth twice, looking like a fish out of water, but found no words, "That's what I thought." She scoffed, "We closed the town to tourists for two months, had to get a whole new fleet."

"I don't know what to say." Hunter was rarely speechless.

"Nothing to say." She shrugged, "We are resilient, broken, but at least we are all together." She smiled lightly and Hunter sighed losing himself in his thoughts. They sat in comfortable silence, no pizza left, sipping beers. A bell rang out as the water lapped against the docks loudly, signaling an incoming boat. Shay saluted to the boat and the bell rang out again.

"Late for fishing isn't it?" Hunter questioned.

"Not for everyone." Shay smirked tipping her beer bottle back to drain it.

Hunter waltzed into the restaurant at noon the next day, same black pea coat, different cashmere scarf. "Catch of the Day" was a quaint, yet well-visited restaurant that had been in Hunter's family for decades. They prided themselves on locally sourced seafood specials and their decor supported that. Locals and tourists alike frequented the restaurant, the only table service restaurant in their tiny town, despite their close proximity to finer establishments in their neighboring city. Round wood tables scattered across the dining room, booths lined the back wall, and a bar flanked the cash register, allowing those who chose to adorn the bar stools a peek into their busy kitchen. The place was unusually quiet, no one behind the counter, tables all empty.

"What the fuck?" Hunter mumbled to himself thumbing his eyebrows in frustration and rang the bell at the register.

"Coming sorry!" Katie called tossing a towel over her shoulder walking out from the kitchen, "Ugh what do you want Hunter?" She grumbled popping her jean clad hip out to the side, her peach floral sweater bunching under the hand on her hip.

"Um the restaurant is empty. Why am I here if the restaurant's empty?" He asked, mimicking her stance.

"We're between the breakfast and lunch servings. It's always a bit slow in between, especially this late in the season." She shrugged.

"Mmkay so where's my office?" Hunter asked impatiently.

"I'm not just going to hand you the keys."

"And why not?" Hunter gesticulated wildly, losing his patience as his voice raised an octave.

"Um because you don't have any idea how to run it yet." Katie quipped mocking his tone.

"Hunter? Good morning baby! Go sit, sit I'll make you something special." Beth winked at him, peeking out from the kitchen and Katie groaned rolling her eyes.

"I run a business just fine back home." Hunter turned on his heel taking a seat at a booth in the back corner. Katie disappeared up a back staircase and returned with a thick binder slamming it down on the table.

"You don't know this business." She slid into the booth, her curly ponytail swinging behind her. "You can start tomorrow…IF you are ready." She said turning the binder to face him and shoved it across the table.

"Open to the blue tab, that's where we file orders. You have to call in orders every other week to the first two companies and the third company is once a month on the fourth…" Katie continued speaking as Hunter stared at the pages, the tabs, the spreadsheets. He flipped through the pages slowly, a bead of sweat dripping down his neck, his breathing getting faster. He pulled at the collar of his sweater, scratching his arm through the thick wool of the pea coat he was still wearing. "Hunter…Hunter are you even listening? Hunter?" Katie called to him and he slammed his fists to the table, "ENOUGH!" He yelled louder than he anticipated. Katie jumped, as did the three tables of guests who he had not noticed had been seated across the restaurant. He took deep heavy breaths dipping his chin to his chest, eyes closed.

"Hey." Katie's voice came softer as she laid her hand on top of his clenched clammy fist, concern etched in her previously harsh voice, "It's not that big a deal. Dad may want to do the paperwork anyway." She whispered and he finally met her eyes. "I didn't think this would be overwhelming for you." She spoke slowly, her thumb rubbing the back of his hand, "I'm sorry."

"It's fine." He grumbled pulling his hand out from under hers shrugging off his coat, "I just haven't had coffee yet." He spit out a quick excuse as Beth came over with a plate of pancakes, a steaming mug of coffee and a cup of ice water.

"I made lemon ricotta pancakes baby, hope you like them." She smiled scurrying back to the kitchen. Katie slid the pancake syrup across the table to him playing with the hem of her sweater silently. Hunter took a small, tentative bite of the pancakes and moaned borderline inappropriately. Katie looked up at him and smiled as he shoveled a bigger bite into his mouth.

"Good huh?" She asked and he gestured at her, silently offering some and she shook her head, "I ate during breakfast." He crunched his brows questioning her, "The breakfast serving was over an hour ago Hunter, but mom really wanted to make you these."

"Mm well, these are quite possibly the best pancakes I've ever had." He mumbled, mouth full of fluffy dough.

"You'd get them whenever you want if you'd just come visit." She snapped.

"Like you want me here." He scoffed shaking his head.

Her face softened as she met his eyes, "Of course I want you here Hunter." She admitted softly and he raised his eyebrows surprised, "So, could you maybe not act like this is the last place on the planet you want to be?"

11

"I can do that" He nodded dumbly, "Will you help me manage the restaurant?" He asked and she nodded, "I'm not letting you run our livelihood to the ground, don't worry." She smiled. When he cleared his plate and downed his coffee, she grabbed the binder. "C'mon I'll go through opening and closing routines with you." Katie slid out of the table and led him up the back staircase to the office, which doubled as a storage space. The space was partitioned with a short wall, one side containing a desk with a computer, file cabinets, a short shelf stocked with books, a small couch, and a safe. The other side contained shelves stocked with nonperishables and cutlery, and industrial sized refrigerators, clearly labeled on the doors.

Katie showed Hunter around the storage room and office, she explained and practiced typical routines with him, and taught him how they tracked inventory, both on paper and on the computer. As they worked, he familiarized himself with the lists of back stock, asking questions when he needed clarification. When it got dark, they walked back to the house together, Hunter pulling his coat tight against the cold, Katie forfeiting a coat all together.

"Hey before we get back, I should warn you Mom is going to announce a welcome home party for you over dinner." Katie said, trying to hide her smirk as Hunter groaned pulling a hand down his face. "It's more for her than you just play along, you promised you'd try."

"I said I could, never promised I would." He stated and was met with a backhand to the shoulder before Katie opened the front door to the house. Lasagna was already being pulled out of the oven as Hunter hung his coat neatly and toed off his boots.

"Soup's on kids come sit!" Beth called serving them each a healthy portion of the steaming, cheesy noodles. Hunter felt his mouth begin to water as he gingerly unbuttoned the sleeves of the crisp, white button down he was wearing under his charcoal grey sweater and rolled the sleeves halfway up his forearm. If dinner was half as good as breakfast, he was certain to be in for a treat. He dug in quickly savoring the warmth, the acidic, spicy tomato sauce, salty cheese. He almost forgot where he was until Katie's voice pulled him back in, "Hunter? I was just telling dad that you're ready to start tomorrow." She repeated and he nodded dumbly.

"That's great son! The locals will be happy to see you around the dining room." Jack smiled, though it was clear he was struggling to dine with only one functioning hand.

"I can work on orders with him; this way he gets a feel for it first." Katie spoke as she slid his plate over and cut his lasagna into smaller pieces, sliding it back to him.

"Thank you sweetie. I'm sure he'll catch on quickly. Can't be all that different from ordering for the museum." Jack said eating his food with more ease. Hunter stared at him for a long moment. His father did not even know what it was he did for the museum, what his job was. He couldn't place the blame though, it was he who never shared that information with his family. The image of his father on the ground, hurt, alone, the same image he had had when his mother called to inform him of what had happened, filled his brain and he suddenly found it hard to breathe. He tugged at the collar of his shirt, dropped his fork on the plate, which had already been emptied and stood quickly.

"I uh, I have to shower." He spit out in a hurry, excusing himself from the table. Katie exchanged a quick glance with her mom before rolling her eyes and finishing her dinner.

The hot shower did wonders for his tight muscles, relaxing everything back into its place. Hunter padded down to the kitchen in his pajamas in hopes of making himself a cup of tea before bed. He had brought his own tea bags, his favorite chai tea from a boutique shop near his apartment, but found himself uncertain as to the whereabouts of the mugs, a stranger in his own childhood house.

"Hi honey, what are you looking for?" Beth's voice came from behind him and he must have jumped a foot off the floor.

"I didn't know you were still up." He said hand on his chest, tea bag in hand, "I was just looking for a mug."

"I've got it, sweetie." She smiled boiling water and quickly made him a cup of tea with some honey walking with him to the rustic living room, sitting next to him on the floral print couches.

"I can't thank you enough for coming all this way. I'm sure it wasn't easy to leave everything back in New York for an extended time, so I just want you to know we are grateful." She smiled and he nodded sipping from the mug. It said "Peggy's Cove" in pink script on the side with faded images of rocks and a lighthouse to accompany it.

"Dad's okay right?" He asked quietly, staring at the mug and Beth's face brightened.

"Your dad is just fine honey." She said cupping his cheek until he turned to face her. "His hip is fractured and he sprained his wrist. He needs a few months to rest and lots of physical therapy after that, but he should be back to his old self by spring, just like the flowers." Hunter nodded, "I'll stay as long as you need me." He whispered, surprising even himself. Beth stood kissing the top of his head.

"Goodnight Hunter"

"Night mom." He called back to her. He brought his tea up to his room and settled in for the night.

The next few days allowed Hunter to slide into a routine. He and Katie worked out a schedule that gave them each one day off and some alternating openings and closings, though three days a week they both worked open to close, to allow their mom the days off. Hunter woke up, earlier than he would like, to open the restaurant, his mom would bring him breakfast after the rush died down on his opening days. Hunter took a break each shift to meet up with Shay at the cafe by the docks and they had dinner as a family on most nights, after closing. By New York standards, they closed early, but that did not agree with the ache Hunter felt in his bones. This was by far the hardest he had ever worked. By the end of his first week, he was running like clockwork. Hunter left the restaurant at exactly three in the afternoon and tugged his collar high over his neck, pulling his scarf up to cover his nose and mouth against the frigid winds. As soon as he entered the Seaside Cafe, the skies seemed to open.

"Oh damn you just made it." Shay groaned from her spot leaning on her elbows against the counter where she was chatting with Savannah, the server and baker at the cafe. "Go pick a table." Shay waved him off, she said it daily though she knew he sat at the same booth, in the same spot, facing the same direction daily, a true creature of habit.

"Usual?" Savannah smiled and Shay nodded, "Usual." Before she turned away the bell over the door rang and a man entered, his rubber boots squeaking on the linoleum floor, water dripping from his nylon coat, "Put his on my tab too." Shay winked at Savannah who nodded in understanding before she went to take the man's order.

"How'd the morning go?" Shay asked sitting across from Hunter as he pulled his coat closer.

"Busy. I never knew a one-restaurant town got so busy!" He shivered as he spoke, his voice rising involuntarily, "Why is it always cold around here?" He complained and Shay laughed as Savannah dropped their drinks and muffins at the table.

"You need your own furnace." She said breaking a piece of her muffin, popping it in her mouth.

"It is unnaturally freezing in this town." He grumbled, sipping his piping hot vanilla latte, which nearly scalded his tongue but did nothing to warm him. He was mid sip when the very wet stranger approached the table. Hunter eyed him skeptically with narrowed eyes.

"Thank you for the tea Shay, you didn't have to do that." The man smiled holding up his to go cup as if an imaginary cheers was to happen.

"Thanks for the halibut Fischer." Shay tipped her imaginary hat and Hunter sensed their familiarity with one another. The man's bronze eyes brightened as they spoke, his naturally curly copper hair hanging in a wet mop over his head, "Hunter, this is Jesse Fischer, greatest fisherman in Nova Scotia." She teased and a light blush crept up the man's already pink cheeks as he held his hand out to Hunter.

"Not from around here are you?" He asked as Hunter shook his wet hand wearing an expression of distaste.

"What makes you say that?" Hunter asked, trying to hide a grimace as he wiped his damp hand onto a napkin that laid in his lap.

"Well, most locals don't wear a cloak." Jesse spoke easily and Shay nearly shot coffee from her nose at Hunter's dejected expression of offense, "and I haven't seen you before."

"Well I'm here now." Hunter snapped knitting his eyebrows together in frustration.

"Then welcome to the cove! Thanks again for the tea Shay, see ya around." He smiled brightly, showing off a blinding set of seemingly perfect teeth as he turned to leave.

"He's very rude." Hunter grumbled once the bell rang again and the door closed.

"He's funny. Cloak, much more accurate than cape."

"I'll have you know that this—" Hunter began and Shay cut him off.

"Yea, yea, the *peep* coat is 100% something and more expensive than a down payment on one of my cottages." She mocked him and his lips tightened, though his shoulders relaxed. Her mocking was somehow comforting to him now.

"Whatever, will I see you tonight?" He asked quickly, changing the subject.

"Uh huh, big welcome home party. The whole town will be there." She smiled and Hunter cringed.

"On second thought don't come." He said and Shay tossed her napkin at him gaining a smile from Hunter.

He locked up the restaurant right on time, having finished his closing routines in record time. He shoved his hands deep into his pockets as he walked back to his parents' house, thinking of the faces he may see tonight. Five years is a long time. He knew he would appear rude not recalling every name, but he wasn't sure how simple a feat it would be. His mom had asked Max, the restaurant's chef, to come barbeque and she would be making the sides. When he arrived home, his mom was already setting out bowls with chips and finger foods for people to pick on when they arrive. He scooted upstairs quickly to shower. He styled his hair in a perfect coif, not a single dark strand out of place, donned a merlot cowl neck long sleeve sweater with an asymmetrical hemline that sat just below his belt line on one side and dipped almost to his knee at a point on the other over his designer black jeans. The sweater was soft and warm; he was ready to tell anyone the lightweight wool was imported from Ireland. He pulled on his black leather loafers and descended the stairs looking for a drink.

"No shoes in the house Hunter." Katie quipped and he rolled his eyes, "As if these shoes would ever touch concrete, they're indoor shoes. I need a stiff drink." He continued without missing a beat.

"Most people call those slippers." Katie smirked, already holding a cocktail shaker level with her ear, it rattled as she shook. Hunter looked down at her feet and sure enough at the base of her ripped jeans, his eyes were met with brown slipper clad feet. The sleeves of her long sleeve waffle shirt, one that was probably meant as a thermal, were rolled up to avoid being splashed. She finished shaking and poured him a drink, then one for herself and held them up.

"Cheers to your party" She smirked and they tapped glasses before taking their first sip. "Remember these?" She asked and he nodded.

"Raymond Massey, you got me drunk on these on my twenty first birthday." He smiled at the memory.

"It only took two drinks Hunter." She laughed and he nudged his shoulder into hers.

"Guests are here!" Beth ran to the door and propped it open. Katie felt Hunter tense in his place pressed on her arm.

"Hey, it'll be fine. They just want to say hi." Katie patted his shoulder and greeted their guests with hugs. He latched on to Shay the moment she entered the house and let her reacquaint him with their guests. After an hour, she disappeared, in the yard he had guessed, leaving him to chat with some party guests he was unfamiliar with. Hunter knew how to schmooze a crowd, but this was not the place for that. He fidgeted with the black leather rope bracelet around his wrist, shifting then to twist the black wood ring he wore on his index finger of his right hand, knowing he would need to quickly remove himself from the situation before he lost his cool. He politely excused himself and walked into the empty kitchen sighing heavily, relieved to be alone. He contemplated a moment before digging into what was left over from the appetizer spread. A steaming ramekin of dip sat atop the stove next to an empty ramekin, which he assumed, had once been filled with the same contents. He grabbed a bagel chip, loaded it with dip and shoveled it into his mouth. The smell was distinctly fishy but the taste…he moaned obscenely, sure his taste buds would explode. He was right in assuming it was crab dip, but it was more than just that. It was spicy, creamy, smoky, cheesy; he detected the taste of shrimp in it as well. Whatever it was, he needed more, like now! He devoured half the serving plate and most of the bagel chips before he heard a light, airy chuckle from behind him. Hunter straightened his back, startled and turned to face his imposer.

"Enjoying the food?" Jesse smirked at him leaning against the doorjamb, his cotton blend cream-colored sweater bunching as he crossed his arms.

"Thought I was shame eating alone. Care to join?" Hunter asked coyly.

"Can't say I have anything to be ashamed of, but I can always eat." Jesse shrugged grabbing a pig in a blanket.

"That must be a nice feeling." Hunter smiled tightly taking significantly less dip on his chip now that he knew he was under someone's watchful eye.

"So you came here from…" Jesse began, fishing for an answer.

"New York."

"Why Peggy's Cove? Doesn't really seem like your type of vacation, no offense." Jesse shrugged as Katie came bounding into the room.

"Oh my gosh Jess! You're here!" She smiled brightly wrapping him in a far too eager hug, which he returned happily.

"Yea, heard around the docks your parents were hosting, figured I'd show face." he said quietly and Katie squeezed him tighter before holding him at arm's length.

"Sooo does that mean you'll come to trivia Wednesday?" She smiled but her eyes seemed to hold concern, had Hunter been a step further away he would have missed it.

"We'll see how the catch is." he gave her a half smile and she sighed, she had heard that response before.

"Don't be a stranger Jess." She kissed his cheek and trotted away.

"So you and Katie, pretty close huh?" Hunter asked shoving another chip in his mouth.

"Uh yea." Jesse smiled scratching the back of his head, his curls puffing out as he did, "We're pretty close. She's a great listener."

"Hmm not sure many people would describe my sister as an attentive set of ears." Hunter folded his arms tight across his chest, the muscles in his shoulders tightening.

"Your sis-…Katie has a brother." Jesse said, realization hitting his features, brows raising in surprise.

"We are not close." Hunter pulled his lips between his teeth, "Don't even know who she is anymore." He mumbled.

"So you're the guy that'll be managing the restaurant for Jack." Jesse nodded, the pieces coming together in his head.

"Hunter Davis, pleased to meet you." Hunter stuck out his hand, guarded sarcasm dripping in his voice.

"Right, I got it." Jesse smiled and nodded, his expression apologetic. Hunter dropped his hand and scooped another chip into his mouth before he tightened his arms folded across his chest.

"So you like my dip?" Jesse asked, nodding his chin toward the once full ramekin.

"Your dip?" Hunter mumbled over a mouth full of food, bringing his hand up to cover his mouth.

"Yea, I made it. We had a great catch today." Jesse smiled.

"You should jar this and sell it by the pound." Hunter said once he swallowed, his voice sincere, lacking its typical sarcasm.

"Yea right." Jesse laughed.

"I'm serious. Let me sell it at the restaurant." Hunter said unfolding his arms, his brain running a mile a minute.

"I uh...I don't know." Jess's eyes cast downward, uncertainty clear in his voice.

"We can serve it hot as an appetizer and sell it jarred from a fridge. We will split the cost even and the profit, 60/40 in your favor. I bet it'd be a huge seller." Hunter rattled on, beginning to punctuate his words with his hands.

"I'll think about it okay?" Jesse smiled laughing lightly.

"Think about it is all I ask." Hunter shrugged with a smug smile as Shay bopped in from the backyard sliding the door shut behind her and pressed a cold beer into Hunter's hand.

"Oh my gosh are you thinking about finally going on a boat? Is Jess taking you on a boat?" Shay spoke loudly, hanging on Hunter's arm.

"No, no, no boats for me." Hunter shook his head taking a long swig of beer.

"Why no boats?" Jesse laughed folding his arms.

"Never have, never will. Not my style." He shook his head again, wrapping an arm around Shay to keep her upright after she almost tipped over sipping her beer.

"Go on your first boat ride damn it! Ooh this is soft." Shay slurred nuzzling into Hunter's chest.

"Wait, you grew up in Peggy's Cove, town of fishermen, where boating is a livelihood and you have never been on a boat." Jesse said ensuring his facts were straight.

"Technically not never, just not in the past, say, 15 years? 18 maybe." Hunter shrugged.

"Ok then tomorrow morning, meet me at the docks." Jesse declared.

"Mmm sorry maybe I was unclear? No." Hunter deadpanned and Jesse shook his head smiling.

"You want to sell my catch? You need to know how I get it." He smirked and Shay looked up at Hunter, her chin on his chest, eyes big and bright.

"That is unfair leverage." Hunter closed his eyes and shook his head.

"Great! Docks tomorrow, 4:30 sharp." Jesse smiled and walked out of the room.

"Wait! A.M.? Like in the morning?" Hunter's voice rose in surprise.

"Yup! See ya!" Jesse called, already out of the room.

"Ugh! I hate you, you know that." Hunter looked down at Shay and she smiled hugging his waist tight.

"You love meee." She slurred and he wrapped his arms around her kissing the top of her head.

"I'm not so sure about that." He said unable to hide the smile that played on his lips. He should have been mad, furious with Shay, but somehow the smell of her shampoo, subtly floral and fruity, quelled his fury.

"C'mon I have to get up at the ass crack of dawn tomorrow." Hunter smiled and Shay shook her head.

"Earlier than that." She mumbled, "I gotta walk home." She rubbed her face and he shook his head.

"Stay, like back in high school." Hunter smiled dragging her up the stairs.

"Mmm fine." Shay smiled lazily. She borrowed his pajamas, the soft navy pants pooling at her ankles, his grey crewneck swimming on her small frame.

Hunter smiled fondly at her as she cuddled under his blanket. "This is the softest blanket ever." Shay smiled at him wide eyed as he slid into the twin-sized bed next to her.

"It's my favorite from home. Christian Dior, 100% cashmere. You can keep it when I go back to New York." He said turning out his bedside lamp.

"You're only saying that 'cuz I won't remember in the morning." Shay mumbled, her nose against his sternum.

"Maybe, we'll see." He shrugged kissing the top of her head, "Night Shay." He whispered before he fell asleep.

Hunter tapped his alarm off and groaned. Hadn't he literally just closed his eyes? He shivered in the cold of the room and contemplated staying in bed and ditching his middle of the night boat ride, but Shay was cocooned in his blankets, having stolen them all from him. He got out of bed as quietly as he could, careful not to wake Shay. He pulled on thermals, his heaviest pair of jeans, a cotton blend sweater and hoodie all from his life in Peggy's Cove before New York. He was unsurprised that the garments still resided in his dresser.

Hunter searched his suitcase for gloves and coiled a wool scarf twice around his neck. He slipped out the front door rubbing his eyes tiredly. He walked down the road scanning the dark, quiet streets. For a moment, he wondered why he was not fearful, but there was something settling about the solitude on these roads, flooded with the warm yellow glow of street lamps, a far cry from the hustle and bustle of his city at all hours of the night. Though he missed the city, he momentarily relished in the quiet serenity encompassing him. As his mind wandered, his feet took him to the dock as if on autopilot. He stood on the docks, the cold sea breeze blowing a salty mist onto his face and he sighed heavily, his brain beginning to do its favorite dance, one he could never seem to keep time with.

"Hey! Morning!" Jesse smiled pulling Hunter from his thoughts, pressing a hot cup into his hand.

"Hi uh why…" Hunter shook his head, lack of sleep and a swirling brain clouding his thoughts.

"Shay gave me your coffee order." Jesse explained and Hunter nodded sipping the coffee slowly.

"Mmm thank you." He whispered closing his eyes.

"Let's go!" Jesse smiled, leading him down the length of the dock to a small, motorized fishing boat that Jesse climbed into with ease. He offered a hand to Hunter, who was too proud to take it until he stumbled into the boat, caught by Jesse's arm, coffee magically saved. He sat on the damp wooden bench as Jesse skillfully backed the boat from the dock. Jesse narrated a bit of the fishing history of the docks and the lighthouse as the shore shrunk into the distance.

"So why New York? Why leave the Cove?" Jesse asked coiling a rope neatly, using his hand and elbow as anchors.

"I was meant for city life. It's fast paced, hustle and bustle, people who think too highly of themselves, people with expensive taste." He shrugged, "The art scene really called to me, especially through college."

"You finished college in New York?"

"Mmhmm did my last year at a New York Community College." Hunter laughed despite himself, "Not necessarily a part of my highlight reel, but the year ended up being very beneficial. I did an internship in art buying for a museum company and met some highly regarded people who...took me under their wing." Hunter paused to search for the appropriate wording, "They puppeted me around, but to my own advantage. They knew I was eager and extremely particular at that, so I became someone everyone wanted on their team. I was picked up as an event planner for a museum a month before graduation and the position gave me the freedom to curate on the side and to freelance gallery openings. My clientele is very specific and extremely peculiar, but after my first ever gallery opening, less than a year after graduation, I was able to afford my own apartment in lower Manhattan." He smiled as his hair began to curl against the misty air. "Anyway what made you not leave?"

"Who said I never left the Cove?" Jesse smirked, tucking his curly mop of hair into a knit beanie, still muddling about, tying up netting and preparing fishing lines.

"Oh I...you came back then?" Hunter was taken aback.

"I was gone six years, went to business school in Montreal, got a great job as a CPA in a cushy office. You know, suit, tie and all that." Jesse shrugged, his left hand flexing to stretch between tying up netting and ropes, "Then two years ago I was needed back here, family stuff. Just can't bring myself to leave again." He ended abruptly and handed Hunter a pole, "Now we fish." He declared. They spent the next half hour hauling netting, casting fishing lines, and raking in a small catch of fish that Hunter could not identify if he wanted to.

"What do you sell at the galleries?" Jesse asked, his curiosity getting the best of him.

"Mostly modern art, paintings and sculptures of very odd looking things." Hunter scrunched his face in disgust.

"What kind of art do you *enjoy?*" Jesse asked as they began their ride back to the dock.

"Impressionism, Post-Impressionism, no one wants that anymore. Money's in modern so that's what I sell." He shrugged, "This wasn't as bad as I thought it might be." Hunter smiled as they docked and Jesse stood to tie them in.

"I'm glad you enjoyed it. And now that you know how it works, you can go right ahead and draw up a contract for me." Jesse smiled climbing out of the boat and offered a hand Hunter would not hesitate to take again.

"Wait that's all it took?"

"You cared enough to know the gritty details of how the business works, where the product comes from. You did the foot work." Jesse shrugged, offering an impressed, turned down smile.

"Alright then. I'll have a talk with my dad and get you a contract by tomorrow." Hunter smiled.

"Great. I have to go, mid-morning crew is waiting on me." Jesse thumbed over his shoulder.

"Mid-morning. The sun's barely even up." Hunter shook his head, "Thank you."

"Any time!" Jesse smiled, running off to meet his crew.

Hunter was eager to finish work so he could have a conversation with his dad about making improvements to their restaurant. At dinner, over his dad's favorite homemade burgers, Hunter decided he could breach the subject.

"Hey dad, so I have been thinking about the restaurant and I think there are a few improvements we could make, maybe adding a section of refrigerated packaged foods to sell." He started and Katie rolled her eyes.

"I showed you the books Hunter, we can't afford changes, we barely make ends meet as it is." She argued impatiently.

"Actually, I looked over the paperwork and I think this will help increase profits." He said passing a folded paper from his pocket to his father across the table. Hunter held his breath and Katie stared at their father angrily, silent tension thick between them all. Jack read the creased pages carefully as Hunter wrung his fingers together, nerves creeping in.

"You really think this could work?" Jack asked, meeting Hunter's eyes and he nodded taking a deep breath, "I really do. The people here, they care for each other and support each other's businesses already. Catch of the Day could give them an avenue to do it that's profitable for everyone."

"You've given this a good deal of thought. Even sketched out a contract for Jess." Jack smiled and Katie sat up straighter in her seat, "Jess? Leave Jess out of your stupid schemes Hunter." She snapped and he held his hands up defensively.

"He already agreed to it." He grinned and she groaned excusing herself from the table.

"Let's give this a shot, son." Jack smiled, placing a heavy hand on Hunter's shoulder. As they cleared dinner plates, Katie stalked through the kitchen pulling on a beanie.

"I'm going for a walk." She announced pulling the front door closed behind her. She barely made it to the end of the road when she heard the pounding of feet behind her, as

Hunter approached her quickly. He had left in such a hurry he hadn't even grabbed a coat.

"Katie wait." He called after her, already out of breath in the cold, crisp air. Katie slowed her pace but did not stop. "Why are you always so angry with me? What did I do to you?"

"You just don't get it Hunter." She began and he jumped in quickly.

"Then enlighten me! Because I'm getting fucking tired of this." Hunter felt his temper rise with his voice.

"You're tired of this?! You?!" Katie yelled back at him swiveling so she was almost chest-to-chest with him, "YOU ran off to flounce around New York." She jabbed a finger at his chest and he took a step back, "YOU get to work your cushy dream job. YOU get your own perfect little apartment with your perfect little friends. YOU get to live a life you have always dreamed of, while I stay here, in Peggy's Cove, at home so I can take care of mom and dad and save their business and this town and wait tables, all while YOU never seem to care." She punctuated the appropriate, loudly annunciated words with sharp pokes to his chest and Hunter backed up, until he hit the wall of the Town Hall. Katie was angry, her face red, breaths coming in short puffs, but he didn't miss the glimmer of tears that threatened to brim over in her eyes.

"I had no idea." Hunter whispered, ashamed of himself.

"You wouldn't." She scoffed shaking her head, "You never cared about anyone other than yourself and I won't stand by and watch you take this town, make it love you and leave it in your wake as you gallivant back to New York." She heaved a sigh, running a hand down her face, "What has that city ever done for you anyway?" She threw her arms to her sides in defeat.

"I don't belong here Katie. I stand out like a sore thumb; I grew up feeling like I didn't fit in."

"With who? Our parents? They love you and never stood in your way. Shay? Your best friend until you pushed her away and she still came back to you. Me? I tried to support you until you literally up and walked out of my life without so much as a wave goodbye." She folded her arms, her features tense, displaying her hurt.

"Life here. It's so simple, I needed more for myself. Faster pace, more intrigue, busier schedule." He shrugged rubbing his arm awkwardly.

"So you couldn't come visit?" She asked.

"No, I couldn't." He sighed, wrapping his arms around himself as he shivered, whether it was the cold or her eyes, bearing into him, searching for answers, he could not say.

"Why not?" She pressed stepping closer to him.

"I don't know." He shrugged turning away and she grabbed on to his arm, stopping him.

"Yes you do! Mom talks about you constantly, Dad reads the museum newsletter weekly because he thinks it will show him what's going on in your life, they ask every single day if you've called and most of the time I lie and say you did just to make them feel better. Don't you think you at least owe me an explanation?" She demanded squeezing his arms and he shook her off stepping back, stumbling over the curb. He felt his chest tighten, along with the muscles in his back, as his breaths came in quick short puffs.

"I-I have...have to go." He choked out, bolting down the road. As soon as he turned a corner out of her sight, his back against a concrete sided building, he slid to the floor, knees pulled up, chin dipped between them. His vision blurred and the world around him seemed to spin every which way as he tried to focus on counting his breaths. He gripped at the grass on his left side, spinning the ring on his right hand, a futile attempt to ground himself. He was so focused on the list of steps, the gentle hand on his knee elicited a yelp. Katie sat wordlessly beside him and took his hand out of the grass holding it tightly in her lap. As her fingers grazed the back of his hand, he calmed down and his head lulled onto her shoulder.

"You wanna tell me what just happened?" Katie whispered, not sure she wanted the answer. Hunter took a deep, cleansing breath.

"I have an anxiety disorder." He whispered, eyes jammed closed.

"Explains a bit." Katie said softly squeezing his hand.

"I don't function like everyone else." He spoke quietly.

"I'm listening." Katie assured him rubbing circles into his palm.

Hunter took a shaky breath, "New York has top notch therapy." He whispered, his voice wavering, "Mom knows some." He said vaguely squeezing her hand.

"You could've told me. I could help you, instead of always being mad at you."

"No one should have to put up with my crap." He sighed.

"No one does have to, but family wants to." She said wrapping her arm around him.

"Good to know." He nodded against her shoulder.

"C'mon let's get you home." Katie pulled him to his feet. They walked home quietly and when he finished his way too long, way too hot shower, he found Katie in her pajamas sitting on his bed.

"Hey." He said softly, fingering product through his hair.

"Are you okay?" She asked quietly and he nodded, "I'm sorry I pushed you."

"It's me, my fault. I'm meant to be an anomaly. Too much, some may say." He shrugged sitting next to her.

"That tracks." She smiled and hugged his shoulders kissing his cheek, "Night." She said going back to her own room and Hunter laid down for the night, his brain riled back up again, self-deprecatory thoughts crowding his head as he fell into a fitful sleep.

After coffee with Shay, Hunter returned to the restaurant for the second half of his workday. He chatted with a few guests while they dined, sharing information about the changes he was in the process of making. He wanted to gauge the response, this was his comfort zone, how he scoped a crowd before an event or gallery opening. With Katie up in the office and Max busy in the kitchen, he flipped the sign to "closed" and leaned against the wall closing his eyes, a sense of calm falling over him in the quiet. The bell over the door rang and he mumbled quietly, "Sorry we're closed."

"That's a shame, guess I'll drop off the contract tomorrow then?" Jesse smiled as Hunter pushed himself off the wall. "Tough day?" Jesse asked, raking a hand through his own curls.

"Uh no. Good day actually." Hunter nodded taking the paper from him and led him to the register where he took out the giant binder. He leaned over the bar where Jesse took a seat on a barstool.

"Oh, if that's your good day face, I'm afraid for what a bad day would do to you." Jesse teased leaning an elbow on the counter and Hunter felt his cheeks flush, spreading heat down to his chest.

"Well, if that's all then, you can drop off the first batch when it's ready." Hunter said dismissively, closing out the register and collecting the receipts.

"Actually, we docked early today, and since you're not very familiar with this town your dad's business is about to begin supporting I thought I could show you around." Jesse shrugged.

"Oh I'm familiar, just not fond." Hunter quipped, a tight smile on his face as he counted the bills in the register.

"I'd bet I can change your mind." Jesse smiled leaning against the bar. Hunter glanced up at him, he must have gone home for a shower after work, he didn't smell of fish. Jesse wore faded blue jeans that hung over brown work boots and a green cotton sweater that looked softer than it should.

"And how do you propose you will do that?" Hunter asked quirking one eyebrow up.

"Come with me and I'll show you." Jesse smirked, "I'll wait for you here while you close out."

A half hour later, after finishing closing routines up in the office, Hunter pulled on his coat and scarf and headed down to the restaurant. He found Jesse wrapped up in conversation with Katie who had a towel thrown over her shoulder in typical fashion. She cleared an empty plate from in front of Jesse and kissed his cheek before handing him a brown bag.

"Um hi." Hunter said, suddenly very unsure of himself.

"I've got your dinner, let's go." Jesse smiled handing him the bag and they walked down the road, Hunter eating the sandwich he was given.

"So where are we going exactly?" He asked between bites.

"Somewhere I can guarantee you've never been before." Jesse smiled brightly as they approached an unassuming, one story white house with a grey roof. It was quite big for a house in Peggy's Cove, but very plain. Hunter tossed the empty brown bag littered with grease spots into a nearby trash can and sanitized his hands. As they grew closer to the house, Hunter could clearly see the words "Art Gallery" in blue lettering above the door. His eyebrows furrowed in confusion as Jesse opened the door and they walked inside.

"This is the William deGarthe Gallery. He was an im—"

"Impressionist painter. Yeah I know." Hunter breathed out, in quiet surprise.

"He was Finnish but he actually lived most of his life here, in Peggy's Cove painting and sculpting." Jesse's smile dropped at the serious look on Hunter's face, "We don't have to stay. I might've missed the mark on this one." He rubbed the back of his neck nervously and Hunter shook his head, turning his back to Jesse as he walked over to one of the paintings, though he was sure Hunter's eyes were shining.

"I love it." Hunter whispered, walking right up to a painting of two sailboats. Jesse smiled watching Hunter walk through the small gallery staring intently at each painting, every sculpture, as if he was memorizing every inch. Jesse found a bench out back, leaving Hunter to wander the gallery on his own. By the time he joined Jesse outside in the sculpture garden, the sun was just above the horizon. Hunter stood in front of Jesse, his jaw hung open loosely shaking his head.

"Ready to go?" Jesse asked slapping his lap and standing up.

"I um…I don't know what to say." Hunter said quietly folding his arms.

"You don't have to say anything" Jesse shrugged shaking his head.

"Oh no, but I do." Hunter took a deep shuddering breath. "No one has ever…I've never…" He shook his head, "Thank you." he finished simply, unable to find the right words.

"Any time. Let's go." Jesse smiled nodding towards the exit. Hunter followed him out the gate and down a small path to the lighthouse. Jesse climbed over a few large flat rocks near the lighthouse that sat atop a small cliff overhanging the water and sat down, facing the setting sun. Hunter joined him, pulling his coat tight around himself.

"I had no idea deGarthe lived here." Hunter marveled, a smile on his face.

"Yeah, thought you might appreciate that." Jesse smiled, "When you said you went to New York for art and how much you love impressionism, I had a feeling you didn't know some of its roots were right in your backyard all along."

"You really listen when people talk."

"Of course." Jesse shrugged, "Not much occupying my thoughts, so it comes easily."

"I wish I knew what that was like." Hunter scoffed as the waves crashed into the rocks under them, spraying them lightly with ice-cold water. Hunter shivered, looking down over the edge of the cliff. "Doesn't it ever scare you?"

"What? Sitting on the rocks?" Jesse quipped smugly.

"No." Hunter rolled his eyes, "Being on the water…in a boat."

"Of course it scares me." Jesse huffed out a laugh and Hunter turned to look at him in surprise. "Any sailor who isn't scared is lying. The ocean is all-powerful; you have to

34

have fear to some degree. Keeps you respectful. But I also am very confident in my crew. At the end of the day, these men and women, they want to get home. They have families; wives, husbands, children. They have someone waiting for them, so they do whatever they possibly can to make it home." Jesse spoke evenly, his eyes never leaving the horizon.

"What about you?" Hunter asked and Jesse smirked meeting his eyes.

"What about me?"

"Who is waiting for you at home?" He asked and the smirk slowly melted from Jesse's face, turning back to the horizon. His skin glowed orange in the light of the slowly sinking sun as he leaned back on his elbows against the rocks. The motion of the water and the reflection of the sun casting fast moving glow and shadow on his face, his features growing hard.

"No one." Jesse breathed quietly.

"Oh" Hunter raised his eyebrows and Jesse swallowed hard, eyes narrowing.

"My dad was captain of the Magnolia. He went down with his ship in the storm two years ago. That's why I came back to Peggy's Cove. Six months after, my mother took her own life. She knew my dad since they were in grade school, she didn't know how to live without him. Truth be told, she died with him at sea." He spoke quietly, his voice wavering just slightly. Hunter was rendered speechless for the second time that day, eyebrows sky high. It was silent for a moment, Hunter searching his head for the correct response to the information he just received.

"I'm so sorry." He whispered, just as the last specks of golden sun dipped below the horizon.

"Life has a funny way of showing you where you belong. After all that, I couldn't leave the Cove again. The way everyone came together, supported each other. When I couldn't stand on my own two feet, this town held me up. Everything here reminds me of them and I don't ever want to lose that." He smiled lightly.

"Well, thank you for sharing some of that with me today. I have definitely seen Peggy's Cove in a new light. I guess, this town isn't so terrible." Hunter smirked rolling his eyes fondly and Jesse smiled at him.

Shay awoke to a chiming that she swore was a part of her dream. She stretched out under her covers, loose tee hanging off her shoulder as she sat up in bed. Her hair was a tousled mess of dark waves and she pulled her fingers through it as her phone chimed again. She grabbed her phone and swiped to unlock it, opening a text from Hunter.

Can you cover for me today?

She read the text again, the simple request dragging her back to high school, a familiar pit forming in her stomach. She scrubbed her hands over her face and sighed heavily. This was a text she had hated to receive, but grew accustomed to handling with ease. She hoped that her tactics still proved as successful as they had in the past.

Key is under the mat.

She texted him back and pulled on ripped jeans, brown lace up combat boots, and a purple long sleeve waffle tee with a black plaid shirt hanging open over it. She locked up, slung her backpack over her shoulders and slid her key under the mat. As she walked to the restaurant, pulling a beanie over her head, she thought back to the days of making up excuses for Hunter's absence in class and sneaking around behind their parents' backs. She would always leave him the key and he usually would find the energy to be in her bed before she arrived home from school. She would bring him something to eat and they would sit on her bed studying and doing their homework. She never asked, sometimes he would offer her an explanation, but she found he responded best if she was just there for him.

> *"I don't really know Shay. Sometimes there's just no purpose, sometimes I just don't have the energy to face the world." Hunter mumbled from under the covers as she rubbed his back.*
>
> *"Is there anything I can do?" She asked feeling utterly helpless.*
>
> *"I just don't want to be alone right now." He whispered and she squeezed his hand tight.*

She remembered how he struggled to put the feeling into words, how he hesitated to let her in, but once he did, how he would not let her go. She never told a soul and he loved her for that, trusted her deeply for it. It made her wonder, for a moment, if he had someone who would do this for him in New York. Luckily, Katie didn't question her presence, attributing it to her brother's need for a lazy day off, despite Shay's excuse of Hunter having fallen ill. Shay picked up shifts at the restaurant from time to time, so she fell right into step with Katie. She hadn't heard from Hunter again and managed to become distracted with the busy influx of guests throughout the day. Shay had just served a table with baskets of crab cakes and fries when the bell over the door rang and Jesse walked in carrying a crate. She gave him a quick wave and he nodded in acknowledgement before taking a seat at the bar near the register. Shay joined him, ringing in her next order before she pulled the pencil from behind her ear and leaned on the counter across from him.

"What can I get ya Fischer?"

"I'm actually here to see Hunter. I have a drop off." He smiled, elbowing the crate next to him.

"Oh, uh, he's not here. I'm covering for him." Shay shrugged nonchalantly.

"Everything okay?" He asked raising his eyebrows, "I texted him a couple of times this morning and he hasn't answered."

"Yea, yea, he's just sick. Stomach bug." She nodded, "Let me grab you something to eat while I figure out what to do with this." She gestured at the crate and disappeared into the kitchen. Shay returned quickly with a bowl of seafood chowder and a piping hot roll.

"Katie is on her way down, she'll take this and stock it in the fridge upstairs for Hunter to go through tomorrow." Shay smiled as he dipped a piece of the roll into the soup.

"You sure everything's okay?" Jesse was skeptical, something not sitting right with him.

"Mmhmm" Shay let out a breath and smiled at him, "Everything's fine."

"Okay, well this is a sample." He reached into the crate and pulled out one container with Hunter's name scrawled on top and a small bag of bagel chips. "It's something I tried out. Smoked salmon and goat cheese dip. He seemed to enjoy the chips at the party and I thought if the smoked crab sells well then this could be next. Just, can you make sure he gets it?" He asked, a half smile playing on his face. Shay caught his eyes and smiled nodding her head.

"I will, promise."

After closing the restaurant with Katie, Shay grabbed her to go bag, bid Katie and Max goodnight and walked back home. She found her house just as she left it that morning, dark and quiet. She grabbed a water bottle and made her way upstairs. As she suspected, there was a lump under her sheets that rose and fell in a steady rhythm. She leaned against her door frame and smiled softly, relieved that he had ended up there.

"You awake under there?" She asked and was met with a muffled groan. She smiled, tossing the bag on her desk and sat on the bed beside him. She could tell by how much space he took up that he was wound into a tight ball, even his head under the covers. She patted what she guessed to be his arm.

"C'mon I've got fries." Shay shook him gently and pulled the covers down. His typically well-styled hair was a mess of waves and he had dark circles under his eyes. Shay's eyes displayed her concern, but she showed no more emotion. "Sit up for me, you've been horizontal long enough." She nudged him. Hunter groaned at her again, but slowly pulled himself up, so he was leaning against the pillows propped against her headboard. "There you go, now drink." Shay uncapped the water bottle and pressed it into his palm, smiling as he took a slow tentative sip before finally opening his eyes. Shay sighed quietly, his normally expressive eyes were dark, empty, helpless. That always got her the most. She pulled out a basket of fries and placed them on his lap. She practically held her breath waiting for him to go at it, knowing he could opt to pass on eating all together on one of these days. She let out her breath as soon as the first fry popped in his mouth. She pushed back his messy hair and as his eyes met hers, she smiled brightly.

"Today was a busy one. Crab cakes sold out half-way through the dinner rush." She told him, stealing a fry from his basket and was met with a lazy smile, one corner of his mouth quirking up. "So your new buddy stopped by to drop off the crab dips you'll be selling and brought you a little something." She got up to dig through her backpack as Hunter tilted his head, a questioning look on his face. She handed him the container with his name on it in sloppy handwriting and the bag of bagel chips. "It's goat cheese and smoked salmon? I think that's what he said." She shrugged sitting on the bed by his knee, facing him as she bit into her turkey club. She found it hard to miss the smile playing on his lips as he opened the bag and dipped in a chip. They ate in comfortable silence and she cleared up and changed into pajamas when they finished. She slid into bed with Hunter and after settling on reruns of Chopped, she set her laptop at their feet and pressed play. Shay leaned back against her headboard fingering through Hunter's hair, his head in her lap.

"Thank you, for today." Hunter whispered, his voice rough from disuse.

"Always. I've got your back." She smiled, then bit her lip thoughtfully, "Can I ask you a question?"

"Mmmm."

"You don't have to answer, I just…I couldn't help but wonder…do you have someone, like in New York? Someone to, you know, cover for you?" She hesitated unsure how he would react, but the thought had been haunting her all day.

"Mm don't need people when you have good uppers." He mumbled and she sucked in a short breath. "Um and no, to answer your question." Hunter whispered and Shay shook her head, pulling her lips between her teeth.

"You coming to the holiday town hall later?" Shay asked Hunter over their regular coffees, a plate with a toasted bagel between them.

"Um no. I didn't become a cheerleader for this place overnight, take it down a notch."

"It's important Hunter. Everyone gets their job for the season." Shay argued.

"You are making this sound so incredibly intriguing, by all means continue." Hunter smirked as the bell to the cafe rang and Jesse walked in ordering his drink and lunch.

"I bet Jesse will agree with me. Hey Jess!" Shay smiled, waving him over and Hunter rolled his eyes as Jesse joined them.

"Afternoon, what's up?"

"Hunter doesn't want to go to the holiday town hall. Tell him he's wrong." Shay said.

"He shouldn't go." Jesse said shaking his head and Shay blanched.

"Hah!" Hunter pointed at her victoriously.

"Wait what?" Shay asked shocked.

"He shouldn't go. He won't be any help with this Shay." Jesse folded his arms and bit back a smirk, schooling his expression.

"That's right! Wait." Hunter looked at Jesse offended.

"He doesn't know how the town runs or what holiday spirit is like here. I'm sure it's very different from New York and he won't understand what we want to accomplish to gain some holiday cheer in this broken town." Jesse continued, eliciting a giggle from Shay and Hunter huffed out an annoyed breath, his eyebrows knit together.

"Hold on just a second." Hunter said the pitch of his voice rising. "I know exactly what this town needs for the holidays and I will prove it to you." He said storming out of the cafe.

"See you at town hall." Jesse saluted Shay walking back to the docks as Shay leaned back in her seat laughing.

Hunter sat next to Shay during the evening town hall fidgeting with his ring, the friction of the wood on his finger begging to ground him, his knee bouncing uncontrollably. Shay placed a hand on his knee and smiled at him.

"You don't have to do this." She said and he nodded.

"I know, but I have something to prove." He said quietly. His name was called from the list of volunteers to present a proposal. He stood up bringing his proposal up to the counsel. He cleared his throat and twisted the ring on his right hand nervously. Hunter took a deep breath and began speaking slowly, deliberately. "I propose a Festival of Holidays to be held at the wharf. We can feature booths that sell locally sourced food, crafts, and gifts. We can have music and dancing with an entry fee that 100% goes back to the town. Catch of the Day will foot the bill for the fees and decor and in return will ask for 5% of the night's profits from each booth. Additionally each vendor will choose one item from their stock and donate the profit on that item to the town. Anyone who wants to sell their products in the restaurant, can discuss a contract with me at the close of the festival." Hunter sounded composed but it was the most nervous he had ever been giving a proposal as his sweaty palms indicated.

"Thank you Mr. Davis." was the response he heard before the next name was called. Hunter held his breath and quietly exited town hall. He leaned against the wall on the side of the building, eyes closed breathing heavily. Hunter gripped his scarf in tight fists as he rode out the panic attack, until his breaths evened out. He wasn't sure how long he was there but soon the town hall emptied.

"You did it." Jesse smiled smugly standing in front of him. "They accepted your proposal. The counsel loved it." Hunter glared at him. "I knew you could do it all along." Jesse offered a smug smile, hands on his hips.

"Regardless of my incredible distaste for Christmas since moving to New York, no one knows broken like I do." Hunter said in a self-deprecatory tone.

"What's that supposed to mean?" Jesse asked quirking an eyebrow and Hunter sighed heavily taking a moment to decide what he was willing to share.

"I moved to New York to make something of my life. What I turned it into is nothing short of a disaster. Sure my professional life is booming, but personally pfft." He scoffed shaking his head. "I got swept up in it all at first, the private parties, the VIP treatment, the buzz. Then it slowly crumbled around me." He admitted before he could stop himself.

"Sometimes, no matter how many people you're surrounded by, it's as if you're alone." Jesse said leaning against the wall next to Hunter who glanced at him.

"I deserve what I've been handed." Hunter whispered.

"I doubt that. Do you think that I deserve what happened to me?" Jesse asked and Hunter gasped quietly.

"That is...absolutely not! Very different situation." Hunter shook him off with a wave of his hand. "Definitely different. Money, clout, connections, they have their pull. Some people will do anything for it and I am one of those people." He continued and Jesse nodded, listening. Hunter shocked himself as the words kept tumbling out, "You do what you need to, to get where you want to be. Whatever is asked, no matter what. You step on people and people step on you, then you move on, because people don't matter anyway." Hunter laughed joylessly rubbing his face, "I have to go." He pushed himself off the wall and started to run, but Jesse caught his arm quickly.

"Wait! You may not realize it yet, but people do matter Hunter." Jesse said and it froze Hunter for a moment before he yanked his arm out of Jesse's grasp and bolted for his parents' house.

Hunter was congratulated by everyone he saw in the town. His parents were excited and Katie even seemed to tolerate him more. He was floating.

"Soup's on." Katie smiled sitting opposite him in a booth, each of them with a stack of pancakes.

"No comment about me wanting pancakes for dinner?" He smirked, he had just closed up the safe and came looking for food.

"Not today brother. You're trying to help the town, you're turning yourself around. I'm proud of you." She smiled, grabbing his hand across the table and he smiled back at her shoveling pieces of pancake into his mouth. "You've been hanging out with Shay and Jesse a lot, I'm glad we share the same friends, they're amazing people." Katie smiled and Hunter nodded, mouth full, "So I wanted to ask you, I know it's only a few more months that you're here, but would you want to join our trivia team?" She asked, a hopeful smile on her face and Hunter couldn't help but smile in return.

"Really?" He asked and she nodded.

"Mmhmm we talked about it and we think you'd be a great addition to the team. One of the other fishermen who was on the team, his wife just had a baby so he can't play anymore and we want you to take the spot."

"Wow yeah sure! Absolutely." Hunter nodded vigorously, smiling brightly at her. "If you would've asked me just two months ago if I would ever be excited for trivia it would have been a hard no." He said and Katie giggled.

"See, I told you you're changing." She smiled clearing their plates and he stopped her.

"Why don't I help you clean tonight." He suggested and Katie narrowed her eyes skeptically. "You've been better to me than I deserve. I also may need to enlist your help in the festival." He smirked and she wrapped her arms around his neck in a tight hug.

"I was waiting for you to ask me. Thank you." She giggled happily. Together, they cleaned every table and swept the floor. They pulled on their coats and walked out together, locking up. They were up the road from the house when the rain began to pour and thunder clapped overhead. They both ran for shelter under a neighbor's overhang.

"We can make it home, it's not far." Katie said as a fog-horn sounded and Hunter's stomach turned.

"Wait Katie, what about the boats?" He asked quickly.

"They still float in the rain." She said nonchalantly and he gripped her arm as the wind picked up.

"I have a bad feeling. What if they didn't know it was coming?" He asked, eyes wide.

"They know what they're doing Hunter. What happened two years ago, it was a freak accident. They're better equipped than ever." She assured him and he shook his head backing up. She groaned as he ran off in the direction of the docks, rain beating down sideways, dragged by the wind. Hunter felt his stomach flip again. He couldn't stand in the rain so he waited in the cafe.

"I've got your coffee Hunter." Savannah smiled placing his hot cup on the counter next to another.

"Thanks." He smiled sipping it slowly. "What's this?" He asked nodding at the second cup

"For Jess." Savannah smiled brightly, "He always comes in for a piping hot tea after a rough weather day." She said and Hunter paid for both beverages, and took a breath. Being with Savannah seemed like a bright calm against the raging winds outside. It was not long before boats started docking, men overflowing from the hulls to tie the boats in place and haul their catch from the netting. It wasn't rushed, but well-practiced. Savannah waved as Hunter left the coffee shop, waiting under the cover of the bait and tackle stand for Jesse to drop his key. The docks were almost clear when Jesse finally came into his line of vision and Hunter was sure he was moments from losing his dinner.

"Hunter?" Jess tilted his head, confused as rain poured down his face, large droplets sliding off of his coat. Hunter's hair was pressed to the side of his face, slick from rain. Jess approached him and Hunter shoved the remaining cup into his hand. His breaths were coming in shallow gasps and he was leaning heavily against the wooden structure. Jess placed the cup down and grabbed Hunter's shoulders, afraid the man would topple over at any moment.

"What are you doing here?" He yelled over the pounding rain.

"I...I want to make something very fucking clear." Hunter choked out around a lump that had formed in his throat. "You have someone waiting for you too." He said, voice as steady as he could make it and a smile broke out on Jesse's face. Hunter let out a relieved sob and before he could think, Jesse's lips were on his, soft and sweet. Hunter sighed into the kiss, his body relaxing, despite his still shaking hands. They pulled apart slowly eyes locked on one another, a grin slowly spreading on Jesse's face. They were shaken from the moment by a particularly loud crack of thunder and a lightning bolt that seemed too close for comfort.

"Come on, I'm not far." Jess grabbed Hunter's hand and quickly led him off in the opposite direction of the lighthouse through the wharf. On the far end of the wharf, just steps off the planked walkway, stood a small building with four condominiums, newer construction than most of the buildings in the town. Jesse fumbled to detach his keys from his belt loop, where they were connected by means of Carabiner, using one hand, his other hand clutching Hunter's as if the man would disappear if he let go. He could feel the tremble of Hunter's hand pressed against his own palm and his heart sped up, pounding against his chest. Jesse unlocked his door and slowly dragged Hunter inside. The moment he clicked the lock, he pressed Hunter between himself and the door and found his lips again. Hands still intertwined, Jesse pressed the palm of his opposite hand to Hunters shoulder squeezing gently as Hunters arm snaked around his waist. Their hands disconnected for a moment so they could both shrug off their coats, which landed in a wet heap at their feet. Jesse toed off his rubber-coated boots and Hunter did the same with his sneakers, their hands finding one another again, fingers intertwining. Their lips met once more, Jesse's hand cupping the back of Hunter's neck, pulling him in as he sidestepped their wet coats and shoes, walking backwards toward his bedroom. Hunter tugged at the hem of Jesse's damp sweater.

"Off." He mumbled against Jesse's lips. As Jesse raised his arms, Hunter pulled the sweater off, undershirt coming along with it. Hunter bit lightly on Jesse's bottom lip as his hands skimmed greedily over the newly exposed skin, landing on the braided belt at Jess's hips. Hunter undid the belt and snapped it out of the loops in a practiced motion, dropping it unceremoniously to the floor. As they crossed the threshold to Jesse's room Hunter took a step back to peel off his own, sopping wet sweater and tee shirt, shimmying out of his jeans as Jess did the same. Jess stood straight up and locked eyes with Hunter, who smirked devilishly, his hands gripped Jesse's hips and pulled him in close, kissing him fervently. Jess took a surprised step backward and his knees buckled as he hit the bed, pulling Hunter down on top of him. Their kisses and touches grew heated as they scooted up on the bed together.

Hunter woke up surrounded by darkness, the rumble of thunder still present in the distance. He took a moment to evaluate his surroundings, waking up in an unfamiliar bed was not something Hunter did, ever. He was meticulous about leaving before falling asleep. A strike of lightening illuminated the room and he suddenly felt wide-awake.

"*Fuck*" he whispered to himself, running a hand through his hair. "*Fuck, fuck, fuck*" Hunter slid out from under the sheets as quietly as he could, finding his boxer briefs quickly on the floor and pulled them on. He reached for his pants and grimaced finding them still wet, crumpled on the floor. Hunter cursed under his breath once more and yelped loudly as a hand clasped around his wrist.

"Where you going?" Jesse rasped quietly, his voice rough with sleep.

"Uh back to my parents" Hunter snarked, twisting his hand to release himself from Jesse's grip as he reached for his jeans once more.

"Stay" Jesse whispered, searching for Hunter's eyes in the dark. Hunter swallowed hard, his heart pounding against his chest.

"N-no. Mm mmm. Nope." Hunter shook his head, eyes closed in defiance, "I don't do sleepovers."

"Please, just stay." Hunter's breath hitched in his chest, Jesse's thumb rubbing gently over his trapped wrist. His eyes raked slowly up Jesse's arm to meet his eyes, his warm chestnut eyes, lit up with each strike of lightening. Hunter bit his lip and nodded his head, something inexplicably crumbling his resolve. He slid back under the covers as Jesse's hand moved from his wrist to lace their fingers together. Jesse offered a warm half smile, "G'night Hunter" He said softly and Hunter sighed heavily, falling back to sleep before his mind could catch up with him.

Hunter spotted Shay seated in a bar stool among the craze of the breakfast rush. He took orders, entering them in the system like a pro, he and Katie dancing around each other like the well-oiled machine they had become in the past couple of months. When all tables had been addressed, he leaned on his elbows over the counter to face Shay.

"What are you doing here?" Hunter asked skeptically.

"What? I can't come by for breakfast on a slow day? I'll have the French toast please." Shay smiled leaning her chin on her hand as she slid the menu back to Hunter.

"Fine. No check-in's today?" He asked as he punched in her order.

"Nope, but we are at full occupancy next week for the festival." She smirked and he rolled his eyes, disappearing into the kitchen to deliver orders to a couple of tables before he set a plate of French toast in front of Shay. The thick pieces of bread were artfully angled, topped with house made whipped cream and a small pile of mixed berries, the smell of cinnamon wafting through the rising steam around them.

"So where were you last night?" Shay asked casually, shoveling a bite of her breakfast into her mouth.

"Um home where were you?" Hunter scoffed feigning nonchalance.

"Hmm funny, Katie said you didn't come home last night." She smiled twisting her fork thoughtfully and Hunter stood upright, his back snapping straight, a horrified look on his face. "It's fine you can lie to me." Shay shrugged snapping her teeth onto her fork.

"Ugh I was out okay?" Hunter gesticulated wildly, avoiding eye contact with Shay.

"Mmhmm I know you were. Where? With whom?" She asked playfully and leaned closer to him across the counter, "You know you can tell me." She cooed and he crumbled forward, elbows on the counter, face buried in his palms.

"Jesse's" Hunter mumbled, his voice nearly lost among the clanking of forks on plates throughout the dining room. Shay gasped dramatically.

"Katie! You owe me ten bucks!" She hollered into the kitchen and Katie peeked out groaning loudly. Hunter glanced between them until his eyes landed on Shay, brows tipped downward.

"What the actual fuck?"

"She thought it was a random, I knew." Shay preened glancing at her nails and she flexed her hand in front of her.

"Fuck." Hunter grumbled tossing his head back into his hands.

"C'mon no more grumbling tell me what happened!" Shay shook his arms, effectively bouncing his head in his hands. "You had sex didn't you?" She gasped.

"Okay that's enough." He glared up at her and she smiled grabbing his hands.

"Tell me." Her eyes shone bright, dancing with excitement.

"Fine," Hunter sighed grabbing her fork from the plate stealing a bite of her breakfast, "Yes and he asked me to sleep over." He admitted pulling a face of repugnance.

"Well that's a good sign." She smiled and Hunter shook his head, eyes closed, lips pulled tight between his teeth, "Not a good sign?"

"No, that's commitment and I am not committed to anything or anyone here in this town." His voice rose, panic edging itself in.

"Or just someone being polite? What happened this morning?" She asked taking a bite of her meal and passed him the fork back, which he gladly accepted shoving in a mouthful.

"Mm." He hummed around his food. "Well he was mercifully not present this morning, but he left a note and a coffee for me."

"Ooh what'd it say?" She asked tipping forward, engaged in his tale.

"Thanks for staying. And it had like a little happy face." Hunter grimaced and Shay giggled shaking her head.

"He knows you're leaving. It was probably nice to not be alone for once." She shrugged and Hunter scoffed. "Listen Hunter, Jess is a really nice guy and a great friend. Maybe he just enjoys your company, and maybe, for the time being, you could enjoy his too." She softened and he sighed heavily rubbing the back of his neck. Hunter knew Jesse had to be lonely, the same way he was back in New York. Maybe, he thought, keeping one another company for a few cold, winter months wouldn't be such a bad thing.

The next week moved by in a blur of extended restaurant hours and a flurry of planning for the festival. Hunter and Katie decided to extend hours when the festival welcomed an influx of out of town guests. Hunter worked well past closing to set up menus and work with the locals who would be putting together booths for the festival. In the days leading up to the launch of the weekend long event, Hunter oversaw the building of the booths at the wharf. Everywhere he went, he carried a clipboard with checklists specific to the day. Feeling very much in his element, the event was not dissimilar to those he held at the museum he worked for.

"So those longer planks are actually going to be for the bar. I want that facing inland with an open space in front where we'll have the high tops we are borrowing from the restaurant." Hunter instructed the small group of men and women who had been recruited to build up the booth structures. Hunter flipped up the top page on his clipboard and showed one of the women the sketch of the layout he had designed.

"Eight foot planks right?" She clarified and he nodded.

"I asked the lumber yard to label the lengths but no guarantees." He smiled as she thanked him and turned to give specific directions to her team. Hunter snatched the pencil from behind his ear and jotted a quick note on the top sheet.

"Don't think I've ever seen the wharf so crowded." Jesse smiled as he sauntered over to where Hunter was standing. He smiled, tucking the pencil back behind his ear.

"It's definitely starting to come together." Hunter nodded.

"Learning everyone's name?" Jesse smirked and Hunter scrunched his face in annoyance.

"There's a lot of people, but I'm trying." He sighed glancing at his paper where he had written a few names of particularly helpful people.

"So, I know you're selling my dips at the festival, but I've put together a small menu of my own for your approval." Jesse smiled brightly and placed a creased and folded piece of paper on top of Hunter's clipboard. Hunter nodded, clipping it in place.

"Yeah sure I'll look it over as soon as I wrap up here."

"Do you want to come over tonight? We can discuss the menu?" Jess asked smiling softly as Hunter sputtered.

"Uh no, mm mm, nope I can't it's so busy here and I have to start so early tomorrow and you know I'm leaving town, like as soon as my dad can come back to work, so maybe we shouldn't do this." Hunter cringed at his own string of thoughts, but Jesse's smile never faltered.

"Okay, raincheck then. Text me about the menu." He patted Hunter on the arm and joined the group of people attempting to build a booth to offer his assistance. Hunter blanched, rooted to the spot. He was pretty sure he had rejected Jesse, yet the man stood in front of him promising to ask him again. Hunter shook his head and turned back to his list, he didn't have time to deal with that now, he would have to get to it later.

The volunteer builders he had recruited worked well past sundown. Katie handed out burgers to every volunteer just after the dining room had closed. Hunter was sure to shake hands with and personally thank every volunteer. When he was saying his goodbyes, Jesse was nowhere to be found. Hunter felt a pull in his gut, a feeling he could not immediately identify, disappointment perhaps? Once the dock was clear, he pulled out the creased menu Jess had given him earlier. The menu was simple; he titled his menu "The Feast of the Seven Fishes" and had one item for each of the fish he would be serving. Seven small plate items with detailed descriptions stared back at him in sloppy scrawl on the paper. Hunter took out his phone quickly doing as Jesse had asked him to.

*Menu looks great. Thank you for all your
help building today. See you at the festival
tomorrow.*

Hunter pressed send before he could change his mind
and received a reply quicker than expected.

It's going to be a huge success!

Hunter smiled, shaking his head and walked back home
for what he was sure would be a short, restless night of sleep.

Katie perched herself on her brother's bed at his hip
after setting a steaming mug on his bedside table. She shook
his arm gently, a smile playing on her face as she watched his
slack features tense and scrunch against the intrusion.

"Wake up Hunter, big day ahead." She said in sing-song
ruffling his sleep messed hair and he grunted in response
turning his back to her.

"Come on I made you coffee." She coaxed successfully. Hunter sat up scrubbing at his face and ran his fingers
through his hair before taking the mug Katie was passing
him.

"I'm going to head to the restaurant and help Max get
a head start on the cooking. I should have our first round of
food packaged and ready to go by eleven and I'll meet you
at the wharf to help set up." She said and he nodded, words
were not available in his brain at this early hour.

"I'm really proud of you. This is going to be the biggest event the cove has ever seen." Katie beamed, she kissed his temple and bounded out of his room to start her day. Hunter groaned quietly, his stomach jumped but he pushed the feeling away. He downed his coffee and headed to the bathroom for a much-needed shower. As he got ready for the day, he reviewed the layout and lists he had created over and over in his head. He wanted to be sure he was not forgetting a single piece to this event. They had decided to kick off at noon for the first of the three-day long festival. Hunter was sure the event had all the makings of success, but a lot was riding on this and people seemed to be very interested. He smoothed his hands over the sweater he had donned and glanced at himself in the mirror. He had chosen chocolate brown corduroys and an emerald green cashmere sweater with a thick collar and three large, deep brown buttons down the front at an angle where his brown tee shirt peeked through. He smoothed a strand of hair that may or may not have been out of place and heaved a sigh. Shrugging on his coat, he chose to forego a scarf, as it was uncharacteristically warm. Hunter arrived at the wharf, clipboard in hand and immediately got to work, checking in on vendors and booths, ensuring the music was being set up and decorations were placed according to his vision and plan.

"Katie is going to make you breakfast, what do you want?" Shay asked joining Hunter at the dock as he flipped the pages on his clipboard.

"Mm not hungry." He grumbled around the pencil in his mouth, the jump of his stomach had become summersaults.

"Sure, so waffles will probably be fine right? Some bacon, maybe a few sunny side up eggs." Shay smirked, she knew all of his favorites, she also knew he would never turn down food. This left her surprised when he denied the meal a second time.

"Mm mm nope. Not hungry." He mumbled, the thought of that much food actually nauseating him. Before she could protest again he turned on his heel to meet the woman behind them. "Hey Nancy, did we decide on a specialty cocktail?" He asked following her toward the bar leaving Shay on the dock.

Hunter seemingly had not stopped moving since arriving at the wharf just after eight. When eleven approached, one hour until the festival kicked off, he was surrounded by vendors and volunteers, bombarding him with questions. What time would the festival close? Ten. How many booths would there be all together? Fifteen. What percentage do we donate back to the town? Any. How many guests are projected to arrive? Will there be press coverage? Do we get breaks? When will entertainment start? Why is the food so far down the wharf?

As the questions swirled around Hunter, Katie seemingly appeared out of nowhere.

"I need to use the bathroom." He spat out quickly giving Katie a gentle shove into the crowd that had gathered around him and swiftly made his exit. Hunter felt sweat beading up on his forehead and tugged at the collar of his sweater as he disappeared into Catch of the Day.

Katie, left to fend off the crowd, stood on a crate and gathered everyone's attention.

"Thank you all for being a part of this festival, that is sure to be a great success for us all. Please return to your respective positions, Hunter isn't here and I don't have answers to any of these questions." Katie spoke with confidence and everyone dispersed as she had hoped. She kept herself busy hanging Christmas lights on the bar and sent

Shay to decorate the booth that Catch of the Day would be stationed at. They were quickly approaching opening and Hunter was nowhere in sight. Jesse joined Katie with a bright smile, his green Henley bringing out the subtle gold flecks in his otherwise bronze eyes.

"Katie, this all looks amazing! I bet it'll bring some great—"

"Jess this is a disaster." Katie cut him off gripping his shoulders, "Hunter is gone, he literally abandoned me with all of this and took his fucking checklist with him. I have no idea where anyone is supposed to be or what else has to be done."

"Okay relax. Where did he go?" Jesse asked.

"Bathroom, like a half hour ago. He's not coming back. I should have fucking known." She grumbled twisting her hair and letting her loose curls fall over her shoulders again.

"Alright, well everything looks great. If nothing changes, you'll be fine. I will go try to find the lists and grab my stock from the restaurant okay?" Jesse smiled trying to reassure her and she nodded.

"Yeah okay." She said and Jess jogged over to the restaurant. He quickly located Hunter's discarded clipboard on the bar and snapped pictures of the lists, texting them to Katie.

This should be all you need. I'll be right there.

As he walked to the new refrigerator located in the dining room where his dips were housed for sale, he heard a quick gasp and froze on the spot. Silence followed, but as he moved again small choked sounds drifted through the empty dining room again. Jess turned to the direction of the sounds and followed them up to the office. He pushed open the door that had only been half-heartedly closed to find Hunter seated on the small couch in the office, feet firmly planted on the floor, but knees visibly shaking, head tipped forward, hands clasped tightly behind his neck. Hunter's coat had been thrown to the ground in a heap and a small orange pill bottle was rolling on its' side next to the coat. The deafening silence was broken by another loud ragged breath, the sound coming from Hunter who was visibly struggling to breathe. Jess grabbed the pill bottle, thinking he may need its' contents and slid to his knees in front of Hunter. He quickly read the bottle labeled with a patient name he did not recognize. He placed the bottle on the ground and focused his attention on Hunter.

"Hunter," Jess spoke his name in a whisper, but that did not stop the other man from jumping in surprise and letting go of his neck, clenching his fists and his eyes tighter. "It's Jess. You're having a panic attack. I need you to breathe slowly." Jess spoke softly, his tone calm and even. Hunter continued to take in small quick gasps of air, his fists shaking hard where they rested on his own thighs. "Okay, I uh I'm going to touch you Hunter." Jess announced clearly, giving a moment before he placed his hands on Hunters knees, rubbing gently before he slid his hands onto Hunters fists. He squeezed them tight and slid his hands halfway up to Hunter's elbow and squeezed again, then did the same on his elbows, biceps, and shoulders before starting the pattern back down. As he paused to squeeze he counted out loud up to four. Jess counted as he squeezed his way up Hunter's arms, then back down. The rhythmic pattern seemingly brought comfort to Hunter, whose tense muscles began to relax.

"There you go, count and breathe. Do it with me." Jess continued the quiet chant of numbers and eventually Hunter joined him counting along, his breathing beginning to even out. Jess took the opportunity to let go with one hand to grab his phone. He opened the text thread he had with Katie and Shay and typed out a fast message,

I have Hunter. We will be there soon.

He quickly put his phone away and began rubbing slow, rhythmic circles into Hunters palms with his own callused thumbs.

"There you go." Jess smiled slightly, after he was sure Hunter's breathing was controlled. "Stay put I'll be right back." Jess said patting his knee gently. Hunter still had not opened his eyes, but he heard Jesse's footfalls grow further as he descended the steps. Hunter wanted to bolt, to run as far away as he could from this embarrassment, but he quite literally could not move, he was spent, of all his energy gone. His brain felt foggy as he tried to grasp a single thought whirling around. He was actively trying to concentrate on moving his feet when he felt the couch dip next to him, he had not heard Jesse return.

"Do you hear me Hunter? You need to drink." Jess said for what must have been a second time. Hunter lifted his heavy head from the back of the couch and Jess pressed a straw to his lips. He took two long, slow sips and pulled back letting out a heavy sigh. He felt something soft press into his hand, but the words surrounding him were muffled. Hunter slid his eyes opened and instantly snapped them shut again. His vision was blurred, the room around him spinning, the body next to him much closer than he imagined. He took a deep cleansing breath and felt Jess shift next to him. He had turned his body, one leg bent under himself, to fully face Hunter as he shook Hunter's hand.

"...just bread, but you should have a little." Jess spoke slowly and Hunter caught the tail end of his sentence. He brought his shaky hand up to his mouth and chewed on the bite-sized piece of bread cautiously. Jesse waited, what he felt was an appropriate time before breaking off another piece and pressed it into Hunter's hand. It took time but he wanted to be sure Hunter finished the dinner roll and the bottle of water. Hunter rubbed his hands over his thighs, the material of his corduroys prickling his palms. Jesse watched as his breathing started to pick up again and reached a hand out to squeeze Hunter's shoulder.

"You're alright, remember to breathe." He spoke softly and slid his hand across Hunter's broad shoulders, rubbing steady circles on his back. Hunter's body tipped to the right and his head fell against Jesse's chest with a soft thud.

"Oh" Jesse breathed out surprised, but never ceased the movement of his hand. He smiled as he slid his hand up Hunter's back lacing his fingers in the thick hair at the back of Hunter's head. Hunter whined, halfway to scolding Jesse to never touch his hair, when the hand moved, blunt fingernails scratching his scalp. The whine turned into a soft moan. This was a new feeling, intimate but not as scary as he once thought it might be. He never wanted the scratching to stop.

"You're lucky it was me who found you here." Jess spoke softly, teasing him, though the words had no bite. Hunter felt every muscle in his body relax, the buzzing vibrations of Jesse's chest against his temple as he spoke soothing him.

"After my dad passed, my mom had frequent panic attacks. Really intense ones. I went with her for therapy, did a ton of research. I was more than prepared to get her through them." Jesse sighed lightly watching Hunter's head rise and fall with his breath. "Then after she died, I started to get them." He scoffed shaking his head, "I am a routine kind of guy. I research, I learn, I contemplate, I troubleshoot and I practice. Then I form a routine. It was like my body was pitted against me when it would happen. Logically, I knew when it would happen and how to be prepared, but it wasn't enough. I'd have to ride it out, or it would make me pass out and I'd wake up better." He shrugged his shoulders and Hunter's head bobbed up and down, this time on his own accord. "I know it's hard. There's no quick fix for this, not even that." Jesse nodded towards the pill bottle. "Good company is the best remedy. With the right people in your life, it gets easier, even when life gets lonely." Jesse's voice dropped lower, almost a whisper, as if that was his best kept secret. Truly, they were both lonely in some way and Hunter took comfort in that. By all means he should have been mortified, the man he'd been trying to avoid had him all wrapped up in his arms, was touching his pristine hair, but he was so enchanted he couldn't convince himself to move. The strong arms and honest voice grounded him, providing an anchor, while the hand in his hair placated him and offered him comfort, safety, so for now Hunter allowed himself to bask in the intimate simplicity of the moment and come back down from the high of his panicked state.

When Hunter and Jess re-entered the festival it was well underway. Guests were shopping, dancing and dining happily, vendors were smiling, working overtime to keep their guests happy, and Hunter wore a shy smile, his hand in Jesse's as they approached the restaurant's booth. Katie flung herself at them, her hands on Hunter's cheeks.

"What the fuck happened? Are you okay?" She asked and he nodded, smiling at her. She hugged his waist tight and he wrapped his arms around her. He was surprised she cared, surprised she worried. He wondered, as he breathed in the smell of her floral shampoo, if she worried about him when he was in New York. The thought was fleeting as she pulled back and smiled up at him.

"You must be hungry. I have waffles come on." Katie took his hand dragging him to the booth and served him and Jesse each a plate of waffles.

"Shay has your booth covered Jess. Thank you." Katie smiled rubbing his arm and winked at him. Jesse smiled, kissing her cheek and joined Hunter at one of the high tops set up for the festival.

"See you got an awesome turn out. Nothing to worry about right?" Jesse teased, smirking at Hunter who smiled back shaking his head.

The festival was scheduled to close at ten o'clock Sunday night, but guests lingered well past eleven and the vendors who ran the booths stayed late to clean up after themselves. Hunter had a breakdown checklist that would conclude Monday afternoon with the same volunteers who built up the booths. It was almost one in the morning when Hunter bid goodnight to the final vendors and glanced around the empty wharf, a satisfied smile on his face.

"Congratulations Hunter." Jesse smiled gripping his shoulder. Hunter grinned in return, his muscles relaxing.

"Mmm thank you. For everything." Hunter said quietly shaking his head, at a loss for words. Jesse smiled catching his eyes and hooked his index finger under Hunter's chin. He tipped Hunter's head up gently and pressed their lips together in a soft, chaste kiss. Hunter sighed softly and slipped his hands around Jesse's waist pulling him in tight so they were pressed flush up against one another in the middle of the lit wharf. When their lips separated, they pressed their foreheads together.

"So about that raincheck." Jesse whispered, his breath tickling Hunter's lips as he spoke.

"Mmm" Hunter hummed, his eyes closed, a smile tugging at the corner of his mouth.

"How's tomorrow night?" Jesse whispered cupping Hunter's cheek, his calloused thumb rubbing gently over his high cheekbones. Hunter nodded slowly, refusing to break the contact between them.

"Meet me at my place...eight o'clock." Jesse kissed him again before walking off toward his condominium.

Hunter was not excited for a date. He wasn't excited because dates meant relationships and relationships meant commitment and he wasn't interested in any of that. Except that he was actually very much looking forward to his date. Could he even call it a date? He couldn't think of a reason not to. Hunter gave himself a once over in the mirror, pleased with his choice of black, grey, and white color blocked sweater paired with black, artfully ripped jeans and black loafers. His day of work at the restaurant had dragged but the minute they closed, he bolted home to shower and put himself together for the evening. He picked up a six-pack on his walk over and found himself at Jesse's door moments before eight. He knocked and stepped back, the short hairs at the back of his neck standing on end as his nerves creeped in. The door swung open pushing the warm scent of garlic and onion out into the cold night air.

"Hey, come on in." Jesse smiled stepping aside so Hunter could enter. He toed off his shoes politely at the door as Jesse closed it behind him. Jesse slid Hunter's coat off his shoulders and hung it on the hook beside the door. Hunter unraveled his scarf and handed it to Jess to hang up as well, then he turned so they were face to face, a smile tugging the left side of his mouth.

"Hi." Hunter breathed quietly and Jesse pulled him in by the waist for a soft kiss. Hunter's arms snaked around his shoulders finding the material of his thin burgundy sweater softer than he imagined it to be.

"I made dinner." Jesse smiled as they pulled apart, leading Hunter to the small kitchen.

"Mm yes. I can smell it." Hunter took an exaggerated breath in and sighed. He hadn't gotten a good look at the apartment the last time he was there. It was an open floor plan with a separate bedroom. The living room was to the left of the entry door and the kitchen to the right with a rustic kitchen nook nestled in the corner. Hunter sat at the nook as Jesse opened the pot on the stove, steam wafting around his face in visible smoky puffs. Jesse ladled the contents into two small bowls and rested the bowls onto already full plates. Hunter craned his neck to see what was on the plates as Jesse placed them both onto the table in front of him.

"What's all this?" Hunter asked, his eyes lighting up as they scanned over the plate.

"So I made grilled cheese, tomato soup and baked potato wedges." Jesse smirked as Hunter pulled his lips between his teeth to stop himself from outwardly licking his lips. Jesse pulled two small ramekins from the oven and set them on the table. "And spicy kingfish dip for the potatoes." He smirked as Hunter's eyes widened. He popped the caps off of two bottles of beer and sat across from Hunter who smiled and shook his head.

"I'm not worthy." He said and Jesse laughed, his ears heating up in light pink hues. Hunter didn't notice, already preoccupied with taking in the beautiful meal in front of him.

"Have to be honest I thought I'd miss the food in New York but you all know how to cook up here in no-man's-land."

"You don't have farms in New York City. The food's not fresh." Jesse shrugged. Hunter put his fork down and leaned back in his chair.

"About what happened at the festival." The topic had been bothering him all weekend and he felt desperately that he needed to explain himself. Jesse was looking at him expectantly, his eyes on Hunter giving him undivided attention. Hunter was unsure if he hated it or wanted to bathe in it. He was also unsure how to proceed. "I uh...I haven't had a panic attack like that in years." He paused again for a breath and Jesse smiled at him.

"It happens when you least expect it."

"Mm except I always expect it and I do what I need to, to stop it. I was so caught up in setting up I lost track of time. I don't know how I was so careless. I'm sorry." Hunter whispered. Jesse sat up straighter, brows knit together.

"You're sorry? For what?"

"I was a mess, it was mortifying."

"Yet here you are." Jesse folded his arms as a blush crept up Hunter's neck bleeding onto his cheeks. "Why are you here Hunter?" Hunter glanced up at Jesse through thick lashes, his head turned down toward the table, and quickly looked away from Jesse's intense gaze.

"I don't know." He responded quietly, having asked himself the same question.

"You like being around me." Jesse shrugged a smug smile on his face. Hunter snapped his head up, eyebrows knit together.

"You're uncomfortably confident in yourself." He shook his head.

"Why not? I'm the only person I can count on and I'd bet that's your motto in New York too." Jesse took a breath, "Look Hunter, I know you're leaving in a few months but what really is the harm in having some real friends to come visit here?"

"Well, I was not at all in the market for a friend," Hunter smirked rolling his eyes at himself, "but then you put this glorious plate of food in front of me. So um, I may be amendable to the idea of a friendship." He preened biting his bottom lip. Jesse stood leaning across the table, lips ghosting over Hunter's.

"Who says I'll be feeding you again." Jesse spoke barely above a whisper, grabbing Hunter's empty plate and walked it over to the sink. Hunter groaned dropping his forehead to the table with a *thunk*.

"Do you even know what a tease you are?" He mumbled and Jesse smirked deviously as he washed their dishes.

"That's what makes it so fun." Jesse shut the water when he was finished and dried his hands on the towel on the edge of the sink. "Come on." Jesse took Hunter's hand. Hunter allowed himself to be walked to the couch and Jesse handed him the remote. "Pick a movie, I'll be right back." Jesse kissed Hunter's temple and disappeared back into the kitchen. Hunter settled on a movie just as Jesse returned with two mugs of cocoa and a plate of peanut butter brownies.

"You're the best friend I have ever had." Hunter smiled cheekily as he ate. They sat side by side until the plate of brownies was mere crumbs. Each time one of them had reached across to the coffee table they shifted imperceptibly closer. As Hunter placed his newly emptied mug on the table he finally closed the gap. The two were pressed together shoulder to shoulder, hip to hip, knee to knee. Hunter felt his muscles tense, he knew what his body wanted but his head was screaming countless reasons why his body was wrong. The moment his knee began to bounce with buzzing tension, Jesse lifted his arm and wrapped it securely around Hunter's shoulders. Hunter let out an audible sigh, the tension very gradually leaving his body. It began as his knee stilled, then his stomach settled, followed by shoulders coming visibly down, and lastly with his head resting in the crook of Jesse's shoulder as his fingers traced calming patterns on Hunter's shoulder. Jesse used his opposite arm, crossing over his body and hooked a finger under Hunter's chin. He gently tilted his head up, thumb rubbing at the stubble on his jawline.

"Hi." Hunter smiled as they locked eyes.

"Hi yourself." Jesse smiled before pressing his lips gently to Hunter's. Hunter slid his tongue cautiously against Jesse's lower lip, seeking entry, which he was granted. Jesse tightened his arm around Hunter's shoulders pulling him closer to deepen the kiss. Their pace was slow, though neither seemed to complain, until Hunter let out a soft hum. Jesse pulled back gently, "What do you want Hunter?" He asked breathlessly. Hunter was breathing just as heavily, their chests pressed together now.

"You." He answered simply before he could let his brain get in the way. Jesse kissed the corner of his mouth, shut the television and dragged Hunter into his bedroom.

The breakfast rush on Christmas Eve was the most packed the restaurant had been since Hunter began working there, even despite the blizzard-like conditions and fast accumulating snow. It seemed as if everyone in town had gathered to begin their day of overindulging with pancakes, waffles, French toast and gourmet omelets. Their specials were even flying out of the kitchen. Shay flopped down in a bar stool at the counter, snow dusted over her beanie and coat. Buzzing past, Hunter almost skimmed over his friend with a "Be right with you", but cut himself off, "Oh my…what happened to you? I thought you were going to visit your parents." He shook his head taking in her folded arms and crunched up face.

"All planes are grounded, so I'm stuck here." She said angrily, her voice cracking slightly.

"Mmkay. That's fine." He said slipping around the bar and pulled her coat gently from her shoulders, unraveled her scarf and tugged off her gloves. "You stay here." He said as she handed him her hat. He hung the wet garments up in the office and delivered a few orders to waiting guests before joining her. Shay had folded her arms on the counter with her face buried in them.

"So I'm guessing this is a cocoa morning." Hunter slid the mug across to her and gripped her forearm until she met his eyes, surprised to find her eyes glassy. "I put a little bourbon in for you." He winked. Shay smiled letting out a wet laugh.

"Thanks. I usually fly out earlier in the week but the cottages were so busy this was the first day I had no check-ins." She sighed, "Can I get some waffles?" Hunter smiled and nodded, "Coming right up." He tapped the order in and ambled back to the kitchen. Shay glanced up as Jesse took the barstool next to her, gingerly brushing snowflakes from his hair.

"Shay? Didn't I drop you off at the airport this morning?" Jesse shrugged off his coat and rested it over his knee to dry.

"Yeah all the planes are grounded, I took a bus back to town. I thought you said rain or shine you had to go get your catch." She teased him sipping her cocoa.

"Yeah well, half of my crew said I was crazy the other half trusted me enough for some shallow crabbing but visibility was no good." Jesse shook his head.

"So what brings you here?" She asked offering him a sip of her cocoa, which he denied.

"Grabbing a sandwich to go, the cafe is closed and I don't have much at home. I was meant to go food shopping later but..." He smiled gesturing toward the window and the roaring storm outside.

"I don't have anything for tonight either." Shay sighed shaking her head.

"Well I will be indulging in boxed mac and cheese for one which I can gladly make for two." Jesse smiled at her. Shay found herself smiling back and nodded her head.

"I'd really like that thanks."

"I'm sorry what was that?" Hunter slid a plate of waffles over to Shay. "You're not having a sad lonely Christmas. I cannot be associated with pathetic friends. Mm-mm. Stay here." Hunter shrugged. "My parents are coming to eat with Katie and I, Max's family will be here too. You two will be joining us." He said matter-of-factly and turned to Jesse, "So waffles or are we in the mood for something else?" He asked. Shay and Jesse both froze for a beat taking in Hunter's offer.

"Uh eggs are...eggs...I'll have eggs." Jesse shook his head trying to clear his mind.

"Mmkay sure." Hunter smiled, vanishing back to the kitchen.

"That was weird." Shay deadpanned and Jesse nodded in agreement.

The two sat at the bar playing cards and hiding from the elements all day. Hunter and Katie kept them fed and hydrated in between the crowds that had gathered. Max, the restaurant chef, left around five in the evening at Beth's request to pick up his wife and kids as well as Jack Davis. Beth cooked away in the kitchen while Hunter and Katie cleaned the tables as the restaurant grew increasingly quiet. Shay and Jesse were in the midst of a rousing game of go fish when the group returned. Hunter and Katie pushed four long tables together so they could all be seated at the center of the dining room and Beth began to set the table and bring out seemingly endless trays of piping hot food. When the last booth of the restaurant cleared, they all took their seats at the table. Jesse leaned over between Hunter's parents seats.

"Thank you for having me Mr. and Mrs. Davis." He spoke softly and they both smiled back at him.

"You know our door's always open." Beth smiled, placing a hand on his cheek.

"Every year, every holiday, or whenever you want some company." Jack smiled.

"We're happy you decided to finally join us." Beth said and Jesse nodded, a small smile playing on his lips as he took his seat between Hunter and Katie.

Conversation was loud and food was plentiful. Platters and serving bowls filled to the brim with honey roast ham, sweet potato casserole, ricotta stuffed ravioli, eggplant rolla-tini, green beans and almonds, roasted potatoes, fresh garlic bread, parmesan broccoli, and fish prepared in various ways were passed around the table. Plates were piled high, drinks flowing freely as everyone indulged in their homemade holiday meal. Everyone stood to help clear up the table of dinner plates and set out the multitude of pies, cakes and cookies for dessert. Katie turned up some holiday music and began shaking drinks at the bar for their guests. Hunter pulled the final pecan pie from the oven and placed it on the table. His eye caught on some movement outside the front window of the restaurant. He stepped closer and spotted Jesse seated on the front steps of the restaurant under the cover of the overhang. Hunter grabbed his coat and stepped out the door, letting it close behind himself.

"Want some company?" Hunter asked and Jesse slid to the side silently making room for Hunter to sit. The stoop was just wide enough for the two to sit pressed against one another from shoulder to knee. Hunter tossed his heavy wool coat across both of their laps to keep them warm. They sat momentarily in the quiet of the night, the whistling wind swiping the snow around in swirling gusts as it fell to the ground.

"Everything okay?" Hunter asked cautiously, afraid to break the silence around them.

"Mmhmm." Jesse nodded taking a deep breath in, "Why...why'd you make Shay and I stay today." He asked quietly staring out at the snow, voicing a question that was bothering him all day.

"I can't be friends with pathetic people." Hunter shrugged nonchalantly. Jesse scoffed shaking his head.

"Okay so the real reason would be nice."

Hunter sighed rubbing the back of his neck and pursed his lips thoughtfully for a moment before giving his response. "No one ever asked me. I spent every holiday alone in New York, and not one of my friends ever invited or asked me to join them." Hunter shrugged kicking his toe into the small pile of snow at the bottom of the steps.

"Why didn't you ask them?"

"If people really want you somewhere they'll let you know. I don't go where I'm not wanted, it's not worth it."

"Why not come back here?" Jesse asked

"I couldn't." Hunter shook his head and blew warm air into his cupped hands in front of his face. "I burned too many bridges to come back. I didn't leave on the best terms with anyone. This time I didn't have a choice."

"Some bridges are worth the pain and work of rebuilding them." Jesse spoke quietly and let out a sigh, his breath clouding the air in front of them, "Anyway, thank you."

"What for?" Hunter asked, turning to face Jesse.

"Making me stay. Your parents have offered every holiday since my parents passed, but you didn't give me a choice." Jesse chuckled softly.

"Why wouldn't you take them up on it? Why choose to be alone?" Hunter asked searching Jesse's dark eyes.

"I don't want to burden anyone." Jesse whispered meeting Hunter's gaze.

"Offers don't always come around. When someone asks, chances are they truly mean it." Hunter smiled and leaned in to catch Jesse's lips on his own. "Dessert waits for no man, and I have it on good authority that the pecan pie is out of this world." Hunter stood up grabbing his coat and offered Jesse his hand. He took the outstretched hand hoisting himself up and slid his arms around Hunter's waist, pulling him in for a proper kiss.

"Merry Christmas Hunter." Jesse whispered, breath ghosting over Hunter's lips.

"Mm Merry Christmas." Hunter smiled pulling him back into the restaurant for dessert.

During the rest of the holiday week Hunter found himself happier than he had been in years. The delicious combination of snowy hills outside, friends, family, and food created a warmth inside him that he couldn't match with a feeling. He knew it was distinct, but was unable to give it a name. For the first time in his life, Hunter felt grateful to be spending time with his family and for the security of having them by his side. He fell into comfortable patterns with his family and friends, allowing them to know him. Hunter began to know the regulars in the restaurant and even could predict many of their orders, having them at the table prepared to their liking before even being asked. He enjoyed his days with Katie and his mom at the restaurant, took his breaks at the cafe with Shay, and spent his nights with Jesse in his cozy condo. The rightness of it all sat heavily in Hunter's chest, though he never spoke his feelings aloud, not to anyone. He was even starting to appreciate the icy atmosphere, colder in January than it had been so far, and yet he minded it less and less.

The restaurant, he learned, was closed on Mondays through January and February, giving himself and Katie each two days off a week, as opposed to their typical one.

Hunter loved his off days, taking advantage of every moment of his peace and quiet. This particular Monday, he had just finished breakfast with his parents in their own kitchen. Beth had made them breakfast burritos and chilaquiles. She was thinking of adding it to the menu at the restaurant and wanted his and his father's approval. As expected, they loved it. It would be added as a special next week. Hunter sauntered up the stairs to his room in search of a particular set of gloves. He squealed in surprise seeing Katie squatted in his room rummaging through his drawers. She stood quickly yelping in surprise as well.

"What the fuck Hunter?" Katie's hand flew to her heart, long curled hair bouncing as she stood.

"'What the fuck' me? What the fuck are you doing in my room?" Hunter shook his head, long arms going wide in question.

"Um you weren't home Hunter." She tucked her hair behind her ear and placed her hands on her hips.

"That did not answer my question Katie." Hunter groaned loudly gesticulating wildly.

"Ugh I needed a sweater okay?" She groaned in response and squatted back to the bottom drawer digging for what she needed.

"Why can't you wear your own sweater?" Hunter was quickly losing his patience, visibly struggling to stay composed.

"I'm going bird watching with some friends. It's cold and your sweaters are warm. You've never cared all the way from New York." She sassed him pulling out the sweater she was looking for, a grey thick knit sweater that looked itchier than it felt. She pulled it on over her oatmeal waffle thermal and opened a higher drawer digging for socks.

"Bird watching? Riveting." Hunter smirked feeling the tension unwind slowly as he looked her up and down. The sweater fell loose over her shoulders and hit mid-thigh, the sleeves hanging longer than her fingertips and she paused her search to cuff them twice.

"Yes Hunter. It's actually really beautiful and relaxing, you should come. I think it would be good for you." Katie hummed happily as she pulled on the dark grey knit socks up to her calves.

"Mm no. As compelling as that offer is, I think I'll pass." He rolled his eyes.

"Bet you'd go if Jess asked you to." Katie smirked, her back to him, fishing for a reaction.

"Jesse's going? Wait no, I don't care who's there. The only bird watching I want to do is seeing a pigeon fly by my loft." He scoffed, folding his arms.

"Mmhmm, c'mon get dressed." Katie tossed a thick, chocolate brown sweater on his lap.

"You missed the part where I said no." He grimaced at the sweater.

"What I heard is you'll go if Jess is there and he will be." She smiled brightly as his ears flushed pink, "You really like him."

"I really like having sex with him." He snarked, pulling the sweater over his Henley.

"Mmhmm yes, that's why you're getting dressed to come." She smirked and he rolled his eyes dramatically. "Hey, for the record, it's nice seeing you happy." Katie cupped his cheek and he smiled up at her, lips pulled tight. She then tossed him brown wool socks and pulled on her boots, her socks peeking out the top. Hunter grabbed his brown scarf and gloves before handing Katie his black set.

"I am feeling generous. Do not ruin these." He warned her and she kissed his cheek before wrapping the scarf around her neck, tugging on the gloves.

"Wow that's soft." She gawked at the buttery feel of the cashmere against her hands and nuzzled into her scarf.

"Yep that is the point." Hunter smirked following her out the door.

They drove twenty minutes out of town, inland, and parked in a gravel lot lined with trees. Four cars arrived soon after and they were joined by a group of bundled people, Jesse and Shay included. Jesse greeted Hunter with a kiss and a light-hearted jab about his "cape" while Shay made a snarky comment about his highness joining them in the woods. They hiked nearly a half hour into the cold barren woods and every positive feeling Hunter was having about the cold tundra of Peggy's Cove evaporated into thin air. He was cold, no, he was positively freezing. He had his scarf pulled over his very red nose and cheeks and the collar of his pea coat flipped up to block the wind. Even his toes, despite boots and two layers of socks, were numb with the cold. His teeth were chattering lightly and he was overcome with regret for not wearing a hat, or coming on this trip at all, or both. To make matters worse, the birds seem to have outsmarted the group and took shelter from the cold and the half a foot

77

of snow they had been trudging through. The air felt thin, frigid, suffocating. Hunter's vision blurred around the edges and he tried blinking it away. When he reached up to unbutton the collar of his coat, he noticed his hands were shaking. Hunter desperately wanted to turn back. He was at the tail of the group anyway, Katie trying to lag behind with him, but he could tell she wanted to be with her friends. He was holding her back, that was not his intention. The weight of the realization lay heavy on his shoulders and stopped him in his tracks. He opened his mouth to say that he was turning back but all that came out was a muffled "Tuhnibug." Katie spun around and told the group she would catch up. She was at Hunter's side in an instant, as he began to gasp for air.

"Hunter, look at me. What's wrong?" She tried to catch his eyes but they were unfocused. She practically dragged him over to a nearby boulder, mercifully free of snow and sat him down.

"Cold." Hunter managed to mumble, tugging at his scarf to free space in his tight airway. She pulled the pack off her back and slipped a white beanbag in each of his gloves to rest on his palms.

"They're hand warmers." She said before grabbing his face in her hands, trying again to meet his eyes. "You need to tell me what's wrong or I can't help you." She tried to keep herself calm, but when he slid his hand up to his chest panic set in. "Oh my gosh, okay I don't know what you need, I have no idea how to help you." Katie pulled out her phone cursing when she realized there was no service. She tried to calm herself and think fast. She pulled her coat off and wrapped it around his shoulders.

"I'm not leaving you, I promise." She rubbed his arms through the layers as best as she could, finding she had to hold him up so his body didn't topple over. His short gasps of air were ragged and rough. Katie heard her name being called just when she thought she would lose her composure completely. Jesse had backtracked from the group and approached them through the trees ahead.

"Jesse, we need to get help." Katie bit her lip holding back tears.

"He'll be fine Katie, he's having a panic attack." Jesse knelt in the snow and began to dig through his backpack. "Keep your breathing slow, put his hand on your chest so he has an anchor." Jesse spoke calmly as he searched and Katie did as he said, wrapping one arm around his waist to keep him upright, her opposite hand holding his hand to her chest and took deep, slow, exaggerated breaths.

"Talk to him, let him hear your voice." Jesse said and Katie whispered reassurances in Hunter's ear. While she worked to calm him, Jesse pulled Hunter's boots off and stuck a foot warmer beneath each of his socks before replacing his boots. Jesse stayed on his knees in front of them, lacing his fingers in Hunter's where his hand lay on his lap. Katie used the hand that sat around Hunter's waist to rub slow circles on his back. It wasn't long before Hunter turned his face into Katie's neck.

"M'sorry." He mumbled quietly and she wrapped him up in a tight hug.

"Don't you ever scare me like that again." She whispered and Jesse smiled up at them. Hunter kept his eyes shut, his body still coming down. He felt his hand being squeezed and then it was let go, limp and shaky on his lap.

"Drink this, the whole thing, before we move again." Jesse pressed a straw from his water bottle to Hunter's lips letting him take a few long gulps before pulling away. Katie placed her palms on Hunter's cheeks, letting her own hand warmers transfer heat to him. He hummed in quiet content before he finished the water.

"Jess you can go catch up I'll get him home." Katie looked up at him as he stood from the ground.

"Katie don't worry about it, I'll come with you." Jesse argued and Hunter shook his head sharply.

"No. Finish your hike, I'm fine." He was surprised to find his voice was even.

"Absolutely not! I am not leaving you." Katie said definitively.

"Then I'm coming too. What? I'm fine." Hunter was met with worried glances, "I want to finish." He said looking down at his lap.

"Alright, but you'll take this as we go. Small sips okay? It's just vegetable broth with some protein powder, you know for emergencies." Jesse handed him a thermos and Hunter nodded in acknowledgment. Jesse pulled him to his feet and they set off walking at a slower pace. Hunter sipping the broth as they went.

"Take this back." Hunter went to tug Katie's coat from his shoulders but she looped her arm in his, effectively stopping him.

"I'm good, you need it more right now." She squeezed his arm gently. They walked about ten minutes farther to an overlook point. The rest of their group was already there looking over the cliff's edge or using binoculars. Katie let him go for a moment to peer through her own binoculars. Jesse was at Hunter's side pressing his own binoculars into Hunter's hand. He brought them up to his eyes gently, cognizant of the chord around Jesse's neck. Hunter was clueless as to what he was looking for, huffing in frustration. Jesse slid one arm inside Hunter's coat to snake around his lower back, his opposite hand guiding the binoculars to the right and downward.

"There, do you see it?" Jesse whispered in Hunter's ear sending shock waves down his spine. Hunter fumbled with the cog at the top to bring the picture into focus and let out a small gasp when his eyes landed on an Osprey nest. He watched for a moment before the magnificent bird took off at a dive for the water below. She swooped into the crystalline river and returned to her nest with a fish.

"Wow." Hunter whispered in awe. Jesse tightened his grip around Hunter's back pulling him slightly closer. They took turns peering through the binoculars, Jesse pointing out another Osprey and an Eagle, then some smaller birds whose bright feathers contrasted with the stark white snow. They spent the better part of an hour looking around and when Hunter turned to look back at their path, he froze tugging on Katie's sleeve.

"What's wrong Hunter?" Concern laced in her voice. He pointed into the woods where two large Moose were walking idly by. The group turned their attention to the two creatures, their massive antlers like fingers reaching up to grip clouds from the sky. They moved slowly with no intention, paying no mind to the crowd gawking at them from a distance. A breeze blew ripples through their fur, the auburn brown hairs dancing about. Hunter wrapped his arm around Katie.

"Thank you for taking me here." He spoke softly. Katie smiled hugging his waist.

The trek back to the cars was cold but uneventful. Jesse invited Katie and Hunter to his condo to join himself and Shay for dinner. They piled into their cars and drove home, opting to walk right over to Jesse's. They kicked off their shoes in the doorway and all removed their top layers, left only in the comfortable waffle thermals they had underneath. Hunter had foregone thermals for joggers and a Henley and Jesse pulled on sweatpants over his thermal pants for modesty. Jesse made hot paninis and everyone enjoyed the combination of fresh tomato, spicy arugula, crunchy breaded chicken, and tangy Parmesan cheese. Jesse and Shay took to cleaning up and washing dishes while Hunter and Katie made themselves comfortable in the living room. Exhaustion from the hike and his earlier panic attack were pulling on Hunter's consciousness. He usually needed a longer period of time to calm his nerves and while their wildlife encounter had helped, his stomach was turning with the remnants of anxiety. He was jerked out of his reverie by the feel of his head thunking down on Katie's shoulder. He mumbled a sorry under his breath, but didn't have the strength left to pick his head back up.

"Lay down you look uncomfortable." Katie directed him to lie in her lap, his long legs stretched out to the opposite arm of the couch. He settled in quickly, guided by fatigue, his head resting on her thermal clad thighs. Katie placed a hand on his shoulder gently.

"You really scared me today." She said softly.

"Sorry." He mumbled in response staring at the waffle pattern on her pants, counting the squares in his head.

"What happened?" Katie wanted to understand, to help.

"I was cold, I didn't think it bothered me until it did. I don't know what it was, it happened so fast. My fingers and toes were numb and I felt like I was breathing in ice. I guess I got scared and it pushed me over the edge." Hunter's voice was soft, trying to put into words what had happened.

"Why didn't you tell me it was this bad?" She asked and felt his muscles tense under her hand. "I just, I didn't know the full extent of it. What if you were alone?" She shook her head trying not to let herself picture that scenario.

"I pass out," He tried to shrug it off nonchalantly, "or take a pill." Katie hissed in a quick breath.

"You, Hunter...you said you were getting help, in New York."

"It didn't help." He whispered, circling his thumb around her knee, the friction, the repetition grounding him.

"So you turn to drugs? I just don't understand." She sighed lacing her fingers in his hair.

"Neither do I. It just happened once, then it happened again. I've been sober since summer, mostly." He shrugged.

"You have to promise me you won't do that again. That when you go back, you'll get real help." She spoke with conviction and Hunter knew he had to try. His life in New York was a mess, if he wanted this, to come back here even to visit, he had to try.

"Okay, I promise." He whispered closing his eyes. She fingered through his hair, her other hand rubbing his bicep gently, feeling his muscles disentangle and loosen. When Shay and Jesse joined them, Shay took a seat on the floor and Jesse lifted Hunter's legs off the couch, took a seat against the arm, and lowered Hunter's legs onto his own lap. Hunter jolted from his half sleep and started to pull himself to a seated position but Jesse held his legs in place.

"You're fine, stay there." Jesse smiled and Hunter nodded in response settling back onto Katie's lap. As Shay started a movie on the small television, Jesse began rubbing Hunter's socked feet, thumbs digging into the taut muscles. Hunter hummed quietly a smile spreading on his face as his body finally gave in to sleep.

Hunter woke up the next morning finding himself in his same sweatpants as yesterday but only a white undershirt left on his upper half. He was in a cozy bed, blankets piled on top of him, his arm slung low over Jesse's waist, head resting comfortably on Jesse's chest. He had no recollection of changing his shirt or moving to the bed. All he knew was that he felt well rested. Hunter sighed loudly and the arm around his shoulders pulled him in tighter.

"Morning." Jesse smiled down at him.

"Mm what time is it?" Hunter asked without moving, he was so comfortable and he was very unwilling to give that up.

"Eleven." Jesse smirked and Hunter nearly jumped out of his skin.

"Oh no! No, no, no, I'm so late. Katie's gonna kill me." He tried to pull himself up but Jesse held him in place, his free arm coming to rest on the arm Hunter had over his waist.

"Relax, Katie wanted you to sleep in. She shut your alarm and asked me to tell you to take the day off." Jesse smiled rubbing Hunter's back comfortingly.

"Oh…um and your job…" Hunter shook his head trying to clear his thoughts.

"I called in. First time in two years, I think I've earned it." Jesse sighed contently.

"Mm" Hunter hummed quietly, burying his face in Jesse's chest. His strong chest, sturdy, comfortable, secure.

Hunter shook his head again, not believing his own thoughts would betray him this way.

"You alright?" Jesse's voice broke through all his traitorous thoughts.

"Yep. Mmhmm." He craned his body up for a kiss that Jesse happily returned. As their lips moved together in a slow, languid kiss, Hunter hooked his leg around Jesse's calf, his hand splayed on Jesse's chest. It was something new, a way Hunter never saw himself waking up, a feeling he liked a lot more than he would willingly admit.

After a lazy morning and a long hot shower, Jesse offered to take Hunter for an early dinner at Catch of the Day. They both hadn't eaten and Hunter wanted to see Katie. When they got to the restaurant, Hunter told Jesse to find a table so he could grab the paperwork from the morning and catch up. As he descended the steps from the office, Hunter spotted Katie in conversation with Jesse. She looked tense, he knew it was his fault. He printed the lunch report from the register and scooped the breakfast and lunch receipts from the blue case next to the register before sliding into the booth. The minute she saw him, some of the tension drained from Katie's face.

"How are you?" She asked cautiously, unsure what she should really be saying.

"I'm good, thank you for the day. I didn't realize how much I needed it." Hunter smiled at her and she laid a hand on his shoulder.

"All you have to do is ask. I'm happy to cover you." Katie locked eyes with him, he could tell she meant it and nodded in return before he got to work on the reports. "You can do that tomorrow Hunter. Relax, enjoy the day." Hunter smiled up at her as she worried her bottom lip.

"It'll be twice the work tomorrow, I'm really good Katie." He assured her and she nodded.

"Wave me down when you know what you want." She said depositing menus on the table before disappearing back into the kitchen. Jesse and Hunter chatted idly as Hunter worked out the reports and logged inventory into the binder he now knew like the back of his hand. He could rattle off goals and projections in his sleep at this point and he was damn proud of it. Jesse ordered a cup of seafood chowder and a lobster grilled cheese while Hunter indulged in his mom's lobster mac and cheese. They shared a basket of fries between them allowing Katie to steal a few each time she came by to check on them, though Hunter knew she was hovering a bit. When they had finished their dinner, the binder long since pushed aside, updates completed, Katie came by to clear up the plates.

"Hey, why don't you come home tonight. I made some ginger snaps I think you should try before we add them to the menu." Katie spoke as she cleared, avoiding eye contact with both of them. Jesse locked eyes with Hunter and nodded encouraging him to spend the night back at his parents' house.

"Sure Katie." Hunter smiled mouthing a thank you to Jesse. They stayed to help Katie clean up the dining room after the restaurant emptied and Jesse left them to walk home in their respective directions. Hunter got right into bed while Katie jumped in the shower. She pulled on a set of comfortable plaid pants and one of Hunter's old crew neck sweatshirts that had long since been forgotten. She knocked on his door with a dish of cookies in her hand, her hair in soft waves around her face.

"Up for company?" She asked and Hunter put the book he was reading on his nightstand, scooting over to make room for her. She passed him a cookie, which he took, using it to gesture at her.

"Is that mine?" He asked biting into the soft, chewy cookie laden with warm spices and moaned obscenely.

Katie giggled and nodded, "Yeah it is. I took it right after you moved away. It still smells like you." She said softly a pink blush rising on her cheekbones.

"I miss you too, ya know." Hunter admitted quietly. "You asked me why I haven't come visit. I think I'm ready to tell you." Hunter took a deep breath steadying himself with another cookie before he began speaking again. "I haven't stayed away because I don't miss you. I left without telling you I was going and then my life went downhill. I have spent the better part of the last five years high on whatever I could get my hands on. I'm not proud of it Katie, I couldn't show my face here. I kept trying to get clean, every time I thought about coming to visit and I couldn't do it. I wasn't strong enough." He spoke softly, his voice wavering. Katie wrapped an arm around his shoulders pulling him close. "I'm sorry. I got caught up in the Ritz of it all, the fancy champagne, the parties, the money. It was all so enticing, still is." He shrugged resting his head on her shoulder.

"Hunter, you still could have come back. We love you, we will always love you, no matter what mistakes you may have made." Katie assured him. Hunter pulled back to look at her.

"You're not mad?" Hunter's eyes were glossy, as he swallowed around the lump that had formed in his throat.

"Mad? Why would I be mad? I'm sad for you, I'm upset that that's happened to you and I don't want you to do that again, ever again. But I also don't want you to feel like that's your only option and that you can't talk to me about it." She looped her arm in his leaning on his shoulder. "I just don't want to lose you again. When you left for New York, I hoped we could stay in touch, but that's not how you wanted it. I understand now, I really do. Please keep in touch this time?" Katie circled his arm with both of hers.

"Mmhmm I will, promise." Hunter said kissing the top of her head. He sighed lightly, a weight lifted from his chest. He was glad to have her to be able to confide in, it felt good to share his burden with someone who was happy to carry it with him.

An unusually brisk day in mid-January left Hunter with a pep in his step. There was still snow covering the ground outside, but the slight warmth in the air left him feeling lighter. He spotted Jesse at a booth in the back, right on time for his day off lunch. Hunter poured him a hot apple cider and slid it onto the table in front of him.

"So what are we in the mood for today?" Hunter smiled at Jesse.

"Hmm let's go with a haddock burger and onion rings." Jesse passed him the menu. He never ordered the same thing twice, switching it up depending on his mood.

"Right away sir." Hunter winked at him before heading back to the kitchen. Hunter quickly returned to the table with a small plate and a glass of sparkling water with both a lime and lemon wedge, Jesse's drink of choice with fish.

"My mom would like you to have the special while you wait, crab stuffed mushrooms." Hunter rolled his eyes fondly.

"Thank you." Jesse dug in quickly. "So you know—" Jesse was interrupted by Katie, "Ooh are you talking to him about town hall?" Katie smiled tucking her order slip into the pocket of her apron.

"Town hall? What about town hall?" Hunter asked. As Jesse opened his mouth to answer, Shay slid into the booth bench opposite him.

"Are you asking him about town hall?" Shay asked snatching a mushroom from the plate in front of Jesse.

"Trying to." He smiled, shaking his head and turned to Hunter again.

"Wait when did you all go to a town hall? Where the fuck was I?" Hunter gesticulated, his brows knit together.

"Sleeping."

"Showering." Katie and Shay answered simultaneously with matching shrugs.

"That is not the point." Jesse grew frustrated.

"Mmkay you all were together without me, but we'll circle back to that later." Hunter nodded abruptly and turned to Jesse. "What did you want to ask me?" Hunter gave Jesse his complete attention, Shay and Katie listening carefully.

"The Festival of Holidays you coordinated brought in more money than the town saw all year. The council is looking to host a spring event that could have similar projections and we thought maybe you could come up with something." Jesse watched the journey Hunter's face went on as he spoke, mildly amused by the horrified expression he landed on.

"I don't know the first thing about this town in spring. Holidays are pre-themed, I can't just pull something out of thin air." Hunter was almost offended by the thought.

"We have time, just think on it." Katie smiled.

"You'll come up with something." Shay shrugged.

"Okay you realize my job is planning events around things that already exist. Art shows with a specific era, sculptors with a clear yet eclectic vision that I bring to life. I don't actually create the event myself." Hunter explained albeit frantically.

"No you're right. You need inspiration, a jumping off point." Jesse rubbed at the stubble on his chin thoughtfully.

"Thank you." Hunter gestured at Jesse, eyes widening at the girls across the table, as if to say *why couldn't you see that?*

"I'll figure it out, maybe after some brain fuel." Jesse smiled popping another mushroom in his mouth. "Tell your mom these are amazing by the way." He called after Hunter who was headed back to the kitchen.

"Bring me some quesadillas please." Shay hollered, met with a scowl from Hunter before he slid into the kitchen. "That went well." Shay sassed.

"Yeah. I'll think of something." Jesse pulled his phone from his pocket, searching the internet at rapid speed.

"I've got it." Jesse smiled and leaned in to whisper to Katie and Shay. Hunter returned with their food not long after and went to buzz about the restaurant. Jesse grabbed his hand before he could go pulling him over.

"Come out for dinner with me tonight." Jesse smiled, his eyes bright.

"We finish closing too late to get dinner out." Hunter rolled his eyes, his shoulders dropping in disappointment.

"Go have dinner with him, I've got closing." Katie slid by on her way to deliver food to a table, her hand on Hunter's shoulder.

"I'll stay to help. Got nothing else to do." Shay shrugged.

"So what'd you say?" Jesse asked as a crooked smile grew on Hunter's face.

"Then yes. I would like that, very much." Hunter pulled his lips between his teeth before tugging his hand away to go wait tables.

Jesse returned to the restaurant to pick Hunter up at five that evening. He was dressed less casual than usual, his standard dark wash jeans paired with a tawny brown sweater, steel blue, knee length trench coat, and coffee brown scarf. He had swapped out his work boots for brown loafers and Hunter had to bite back a comment regarding how handsome he looked. Jesse gave him a wave as he entered the restaurant and Hunter held up a finger darting up the steps to the office. He gave himself a once over, smoothing out his fair isle black and white sweater. He sighed tucking back a stubborn lock of hair, cursing himself for not keeping a spare gel up in the office. He had no choice at this point, it would all have to do. Hunter pulled on his black scarf and gloves set, then donned his pea coat and met Jesse in the dining room where he was chatting with Katie, head thrown back in laughter.

"Ready to go?" Hunter approached them cautiously as Jesse surreptitiously swiped at a tear in the corner of his eye, his laughter settling down.

"Ready." He kissed Katie on the cheek with a thank you and started out of the restaurant. Hunter smiled and Katie winked at him shooing him with her hands until he followed Jesse. They piled into Jesse's dark grey sedan and Hunter clicked in his seatbelt, ringing his hands together nervously.

"You alright there?" Jesse asked clicking in his own seatbelt before pulling out onto the road.

"Mmhmm yeah. You...you're kinda...am I underdressed?" Hunter asked raising his eyebrows. Jesse smiled, reaching over and took Hunter's hand in his own.

"You're dressed perfectly as always. Why would you be concerned about that?" Jesse asked.

"You look really great Jesse." Hunter smiled shyly. Jesse picked Hunter's hand up, placing a kiss on his knuckles.

"So what you're saying is I usually dress like a bum."
Jesse smirked at him. Hunter sputtered searching for a rebut.
"I'm kidding Hunter, relax." Jesse laughed squeezing his
hand. He rested their joined hands on Hunter's lap. Hunter
took a cleansing breath and settled back into the soft material
seat.

"Where are we headed anyway?"

"Halifax." Jesse smiled knowingly and watched Hunter's
expression morph once again.

"That's not really down the road." Hunter bit his lip
and Jesse laughed.

"Nope not exactly. Just found something I think might
inspire you." He shrugged.

"You'll have to explain to me why this means so much
to you." Hunter shook his head.

"It's just something good for the town." Jesse shrugged
and Hunter squeezed his hand.

"Nice try, c'mon truth." Hunter smiled knowingly.

"Well, uh…it's my family." Jesse shrugged. "I don't have
anyone. My parents didn't have siblings, my grandparents
all passed. Peggy's Cove…it's all I have." Jesse gave a small
smile. Hunter squeezed his hand, something tugging on his
heart. He didn't trust his voice to work around the lump in
his throat. Hunter cleared his throat after a few minutes of
silence.

"Okay, let's figure something out for a spring festival."

"Thank you Hunter." Jesse's smile was worth it. A half
hour later, they parked in a lot in the center of Downtown
Halifax. They walked into an upscale Italian restaurant decorated with Venetian masks and blown glass. Jesse checked
them in as Hunter gawked in awe of the artwork strewn
about the lobby.

"Come, our table is ready." Jesse smiled, taking his hand as they followed the host to their table. Hunter was speechless, so taken by the ambience that he didn't even notice their orders weren't taken. Within minutes, three appetizer plates and two Aperol spritz cocktails were placed in front of them. Hunter screwed his face in confusion.

"What's this?" He asked looking up at Jesse.

"So we are not actually eating dinner here." Jesse smiled and Hunter shook his head, pursing his lips. "This is the first stop of the Halifax Restaurant Crawl." Jesse smiled brightly as Hunter's eyes lit up. His grin taking over his entire face.

"Wow. I don't know what to say."

"I figured it would be the best date for you up here in the 'tundra' as you put it." Jesse smirked. Hunter bit the inside of his cheek a bright blush rising to the apples of his cheeks.

"Date huh?"

Jesse shrugged, "Thought it was about time I took you out for a real one."

"Well, I will drink to that." Hunter lifted his glass. Jesse mirrored him and they both took a sip after their glasses clinked together. They shared plates of prosciutto and melon, eggplant Rollatini and crostini with four different toppings. They then moved on to a Spanish place for tapas; coconut shrimp, sweet ribs, and paella, then to a German place for schnitzel and Schinkennudeln, pasta gratin with ham, onion and cheese. Each meal was accompanied by a drink pairing and by the time they had finished in the German place, both thought they were full to the brim.

"I have never eaten so many different foods in one sitting." Hunter leaned back in his seat, hands flat on his stomach.

"Guess the people of New York don't understand the concept of a fun date night." Jesse sipped some water and sighed, fighting the urge to unbutton his pants.

"I can honestly say I have never been on a date that even comes close to your league." Hunter smiled.

"Well, I've never dated anyone that even comes close to your league." Jesse smiled locking eyes with Hunter.

"Aah so you have done this before."

"Not this exactly, but I know how to turn on the romance." Jesse wiggled his eyebrows and Hunter laughed.

"Yeah? How's that worked out for you so far?"

"You know, I do have this secret boyfriend I never told you about, I hide him in my garage so I can have fun with you and not worry so much about him." Jesse bit back a smile as Hunter threw his head back full on chuckling. "I was in a serious relationship back in Toronto." Jesse spoke again when Hunter's laughter had died down. They both stood linking their fingers together as they walked to their next destination. "We were together two years, Greg and I. He was a great guy, a surgeon." Hunter raised his eyebrows and tilted his head inviting Jesse to continue. "He came back here with me for my dad's service. He wanted to be in Toronto."

"Always attracted to city boys then?" Hunter sassed, gaining a smile from Jesse, who hip checked him lightly.

"Guess so. He grew up there, had a big family all there. He offered to buy my mom a house there. I mentioned it once, she was appalled that I would want her to leave my father. I think somewhere in her mind she believed they'd find him one day, that he'd just come home. Greg waited for me, came back when my mom passed, but," he stopped and sighed heavily, "can't expect people to wait forever. I didn't want to leave after that, he didn't want to come here. He gave me the choice, and I chose." He shrugged.

"His loss." Hunter said softly, met with a humorless laugh from Jesse.

"Loss." Jesse whispered the word like it tasted foul on his lips. Then he cleared his throat and pulled open the door to a small Italian bakery. The black and white checked floor and small wooden tables gave a very rustic atmosphere with accordion music to match the scene. Jesse and Hunter sat across from one another and were served a platter of Italian cookies and pastries from seven layers and biscotti to cannoli and sfogliatelle with small scoops of gelato around the rim of the platter.

"Who knew Halifax had such great food." Hunter mused, taking a mouthful of cannoli.

"We are more than just a bunch of seafood you know." Jesse smirked winking at him, the light mood returning quickly as if it had never left. "What about you? What was your relationship history like?" He asked with a teasing lilt to his voice.

"Yeah, not much to tell there. Definitely no one willing to travel to bumfuck lighthouse land for me." Hunter laughed lightly. "I'm not stable enough for that kind of thing...relationships, commitment." He spoke around a mouthful of food.

Jesse nodded in understanding, "So hit it and quit it." Hunter nearly choked on his dessert as a smug grin bloomed on Jesse's face.

"I do enjoy being wined and dined too, just never stuck around for anything meaningful, or had someone who wanted me to." Hunter shrugged.

"So you just up and leave when you're through?"

"You make me sound like a monster. I just know when I've worn out my welcome is all."

"And yet you're still sitting here." Jesse leaned forward, elbow on the table, hand cradling his chin, eyes locked on Hunter's as the other man narrowed his eyes and pulled his lips tight to one side, trying to assess if Jesse was messing with him. Jesse schooled his expression to be as serious as he could, until he could no longer hold back a smile and leaned back resting his hand palm up on the table top. Hunter smiled back laying his hand on top, squeezing once before going back to his dessert, their hands linked atop the table.

Their final stop was an upscale French Patisserie with stark white tablecloths, black and white striped wallpaper and fairy lights draped about the ceiling. The walls were littered with black and white photographs of Paris and candles flickered on each table. They were served crème brûlée, madeleines, and macarons.

"So how'd I do?" Jesse asked, tapping his spoon at the sugar shell over his crème brûlée.

"This may be the best date I have ever been on." Hunter pointed his spoon at Jesse across the table, "Don't let it get to your head."

Jesse preened, proud of himself, "You like your food Hunter. A smorgasbord of worldwide cuisine just seemed like an obvious choice, especially with how you react to my rustic cooking." Jesse laughed lightly. He hadn't initially noticed Hunter stopped listening to him. "I can see your cogs turning, what're you thinking over there?"

Hunter shook his head returning from his reverie, "Smorgasbord, that's it." He snapped his fingers. "We'll host the spring festival all four weekends in April, each weekend with a different food specific theme. People love to indulge... food, wine, dessert. We keep the vendors consistent. Every participating vendor will have to rent their booth for all four weekends, all the money goes to the town. We charge admission like the holiday festival. The first weekend will be ice wine. It's so specific, so Canadian, and it's a slow tourist week so that will be a big draw. Then we'll get some vintners to sponsor and set up a booth to sell their ice wines. We can do food week two, worldwide cuisine, then desserts and the last week, a music festival with carnival type food, real sugary, deep fried crap that everyone loves." Hunter spoke with conviction, painting his vision clearly for Jesse who smiled back at him taking it all in.

"You are brilliant." Hunter finally met Jesse's eyes, earnest, with no hint of his typical teasing.

"Thank you." Hunter whispered. "Um maybe you could help with the planning? You know to avoid a tailspin panic attack." Hunter cringed at the memory.

"Absolutely, I'd be happy to." They finished their desserts, walking slower back to Jesse's car, both laughing as they unbuttoned their jeans to offer some breathing room. Hunter looked out the window, watching the snow covered trees roll by. He had a full belly and a full heart, not fighting the feeling that had overcome him, but also not gracing it with a name. For now, he was more than happy to hold hands with the man next to him and bask in the tailor made date night that had been planned for him on a whim, so perfectly spot on. He couldn't remember a time someone had been so thoughtful and mindful of him, but his subconscious nagged, reminding him it was temporary, short lived, couldn't ever be what he wouldn't let himself dream it to be.

Katie was a little perturbed when Hunter didn't arrive at the restaurant on time on a snowy day in February. When Shay showed up for breakfast and hadn't heard from or seen him, she became worried. Hunter had been knee deep in spring festival plans for weeks and spent most nights at Jesse's, but he was never late.

"I'll check around for him, maybe he's just having one of those days." Shay assured Katie, pulled on her hat and went to check his own house and hers. She returned just before lunch with no sign of him, her texts and calls left unanswered. Shay made a call to Jesse who, as she expected, was on his boat finishing, none the wiser to Hunter's whereabouts.

"He always goes to you Shay, he feels safe with you." Katie scrubbed a hand over her face.

"Right…that's right and now he's…I have a thought as to where he may be. I'll text you okay?" Shay left the restaurant in a hurry, picked up a bag of food from the cafe and waited on the docks for Jesse.

"Here for some fresh catch?" Jesse approached her as soon as he turned in his keys.

"Not today, have you heard from Hunter?"

"No, probably a busy day at the restaurant. He's been deep in pla—"

"He didn't show up for work today Jesse." Shay cut him off mid-sentence.

"What'd you mean? Where is he?" Jesse laughed in an effort to calm his rising nerves.

"So we don't know for sure, but I think he's at your apartment." Shay bit her lip.

"Shay, he leaves after me every day, sets four alarms and…Why do I feel like there's more to this?"

"There is, I'll walk home with you." Shay matched his slow, hesitant stride as they walked to his condo side by side.

She filled him in on her days coming home from school to find Hunter in her bed and how he should make sure Hunter ate and drank. She handed him the brown takeout bag from the cafe, patted his shoulder, and wished him luck, parting ways at his front door. Jesse was skeptical, unsure why Hunter would choose his place to spend his day. He was hesitant, afraid to make things worse, but even still, he took a steadying breath and opened the door. He found his condo exactly as it always was, lights off, everything neatly in its place. He tossed the bag onto his kitchen table and toed off his shoes. He hung his coat, hat and scarf letting his tension go. He knew he wouldn't find Hunter there. He was about to text Shay when he stopped himself. He pursed his lips thoughtfully and padded into his room. Sure enough, there was a lump under his duvet. He shot a text to Shay that he was there and stuck his phone back in his pocket. Jesse sighed quietly, and stepped closer. Hunter was completely under the covers, just a soft tuft of his jet-black hair peeking out against the stark white pillow. Jesse was impressed by the incredibly small amount of space Hunter was taking up in his large bed. Hunter was tall, all long limbs and long torso, it amazed him the size of the ball Hunter had curled himself into. Jesse took a steadying breath, he'd done this so many times with his own mother, he just hoped the result was more promising. Jesse lowered himself to his knees on the floor near the top of the bed, where Hunter's head surely was. He paused for another calming breath before clearing his throat.

"Hunter?" Jesse whispered, afraid to disturb the quiet darkness of the room, only a small bluish glow illuminated the bed where light peeked through the split in the curtains. "I'm going to touch you." He warned quietly, though he wasn't even sure Hunter was awake. The only movement was a slow rise and fall of the navy duvet with Hunter's breaths. Jesse waited a moment before laying a steady hand on Hunter's shoulder. He rubbed his thumb in slow circles, then dragged his hand down what he assumed was Hunter's side and back up to his shoulder. Hunter let out a nearly silent whimper, which could have been mistaken for a sigh. Jesse gripped his shoulder, a physical reminder that he was not alone, then he started to talk.

"So Chester, one of the fishermen in my crew, caught a shark today. It was small, three feet, but it put up quite a fight. Took two men to reel it in. Poor thing was probably scared half to death. No one wanted to release the hook, so I did it. I thought of you, how amused you would have been watching three men wrestle a shark, how you would've turned up your nose in disgust, but secretly been worried about the shark. I got the hook out, barely any damage done and we released it. So happy ending." Jesse spoke softly, his tone even. He wasn't sure it would help, but his mom would always relax hearing his stories. She would say it helped her mind focus when there were too many racing thoughts getting her down. As Jesse wove his tale, long fingers peeked out from under the covers. He took the invitation and interlocked his fingers with Hunter's, giving his hand a reassuring squeeze, the other still rubbing his shoulder. The weight of their hands was just enough to pull down the duvet and expose Hunter's thick brows and usually expressive eyes, now shut tight against the world. Jesse moved his hand up to cup the back of Hunter's head, thumb rubbing over his temple.

"It doesn't happen often that we catch something we're not supposed to, but I'm a stickler for proper release. I've seen men toss a shark back with a hook still in its mouth. That's no way to live, it's against my moral compass, also against the rules. Who wants to pay a fine just out of laziness? My men are great, but they're chicken shit when it comes to sharks." Jesse continued, watching carefully as Hunter's eyes parted to stare down at their linked hands.

"There you are." Jesse dragged a thumb over Hunter's eyebrow and gave him a soft smile. He knew he wouldn't gain eye contact, not yet, but this was a step in the right direction. "Have you gotten up at all today? For food, water, bathroom?" Jesse asked and Hunter shook his head just enough to convey an answer. "You should stretch out a little, give your muscles a break."

When Hunter spoke, his voice was thick and gravely, and so quiet if a car had gone by, Jesse would have missed when he said, "I don't deserve...to take up space." Jesse's brain had to quickly catch up, he checked his emotions without missing a beat and did not hesitate before he answered.

"You do with me." Jesse squeezed Hunter's hand reassuringly, "You take up as much space as you need. As much as you want." He knew it was what Hunter needed to hear, but found himself meaning it deeply. He wanted Hunter to take up space in his life. Relief washed over him when Hunter let his knees slide down from his chest, unraveling himself just slightly. Jesse smiled at him and pulled Hunter's hand closer to him, pressing a kiss to his knuckles. He waited until Hunter met his eyes, they contrasted one another harshly; Hunter's eyes dark, empty, longing, while Jesse's were bright, warm and inviting. Hunter felt safe getting lost in those eyes, for a moment he let himself feel he belonged there. When the feeling overwhelmed him, he closed his eyes and dipped his head, pressing his forehead to Jesse's hand still weaved with his own.

"Thank you." Jesse whispered and Hunter looked up and him in question. "For trusting me." Hunter's cheeks heated with a blush. Jesse knew he hit the nail on the head,

Hunter had waited for him, wanted him to be the one to help.

"I'm going to get you some food. Don't go anywhere now." Jesse smirked slipping his hand out of Hunter's and headed for the kitchen. He let out a breath he didn't realize he'd been holding. He brewed a fresh mug of tea, added honey, and snatched up the bag Shay had given him. When he joined Hunter back in his bedroom, Hunter had sat himself up against the headboard, knees pulled close to his chest, his head buried in his arms, blankets still pulled up high, shivering slightly. Jesse set the mug and bag on his bedside table and pulled a soft, knit blanket from the foot of his bed. He draped the blanket over Hunter's shoulders and slid under the covers next to him.

"Here, this should warm you up." Jesse tapped his shoulder and handed him the steaming mug of tea. "Shay sent this for you, so if you hate it you can blame her." The corner of Hunter's mouth twitched up just slightly. Jesse pulled two bagels from the brown paper bag. They shared the bagels in silence until the mug and bag were both empty. Jesse held his arm out to Hunter, inviting him in. Hunter hesitated before leaning in, his head pillowed against the soft sweater covering Jesse's chest, knees tucked up over Jesse's thigh. Jesse slung his arm around Hunter's shoulders holding him against his own side.

"This okay?" Jesse asked and Hunter hummed his approval. Jesse traced his fingers over the deep-set creases in Hunter's cheek, imprints of the folds in the sheets he had been pressed into all day. Hunter gripped his sweater tight in a fist that rested on Jesse's stomach.

"I got someone to cover me tomorrow, I could take you out on a boat, see if we can spot some whales." Jesse suggested, tracing light patterns on Hunter's back through his thin pajama shirt.

"You don't have to." Hunter tensed as he spoke. Jesse wrapped him tight in his arms and pressed a kiss in his messy hair.

"I know, but I want to. It'd be nice to spend a relaxing day just us." Hunter tilted his head up, staring at Jesse.

"Why are you so nice to me?" The question sounded elementary as he spoke it, but he genuinely wanted to know. He didn't feel he deserved it, and certainly never received attention like this before.

"I enjoy your company, like spending time with you. If I want you to stick around why would I be anything but nice?" Jesse shrugged. He spoke as if it was so obvious, so easy. The words replayed in Hunters head. *I want you to stick around.* That wasn't something he'd heard before, it struck him. *I want you to stick around.* He felt a warmth spread through his chest and his muscles finally unwound themselves. He knew he was dead weight against the entire left side of Jesse's body, but he didn't care. It struck him suddenly that he wanted to stick around too, he wanted this for keeps.

"Yeah, I like that," was all he could manage to mumble before sleep took his exhausted body.

The weather betrayed them yet again at the end of February with a lengthy snowstorm that left a foot and a half of snow pillowing the ground. Hunter found himself enjoying the downtick in temperature as a constant excuse to be close to Jesse, whether they were snuggled up indoors or pressed together, hand in hand, walking outside. Hunter woke up alone in Jesse's bed, as he always did. He showered and got dressed for the day before entering the kitchen to find fresh corn muffins and a note on the table. He sat happily at the little kitchen nook munching on a muffin as he read the note.

> *Hunter*
> *I have to take care of something after work. Will be back late. See you tomorrow. Enjoy the muffins!*
> *-Jess*

Hunter scrunched his eyebrows in confusion. He found it odd that Jesse was asking him not to stay over tonight, even in his subtly polite way. Hunter hadn't spent a night home in weeks, maybe it was good to have space. He took an extra muffin for the road and walked to the restaurant, guarding his breakfast against the sharp wind. He had texted Jesse once without a response, though he didn't usually answer at work. Hunter went about his day, busier than usual, which he found to be typical on bad weather days. People loved his mom and Max's warm comfort food on especially cold days. Shay joined him in the restaurant for lunch instead of the cafe, claiming to be hungry for something heartier, that same pull towards comfort food. He sat in a booth across from her, a plate of crab cakes and a basket of cheese fries between them.

"So what are you doing tonight? Got something special planned? Turning on the romance?" Shay wiggled her eyebrows playfully as she popped a fry in her mouth.

"Pfft, nothing. Maybe I'll ask my parents if they want me to pick up a pizza or something." Hunter scoffed.

Shay's eyes widened, "You're kidding right?"

"No, Jesse's busy tonight." Hunter shrugged trying not to be bothered by it, his lips pulled harshly to one side.

"Kay well as much as I am loving how much that's bugging you, you have to get it together. It's Jesse's birthday!" Shay smiled slapping the table excitedly. Hunter pulled a face, his brows dipped in an unasked question. "And you did not know that." She spoke slowly, realizing she may have spoken out of turn.

"Why wouldn't he tell me that?" Hunter scrubbed at his stubbled chin, a question he didn't expect her to answer.

"Well now that you know, what're you gonna do about it?"

"I may need a minute to think." Hunter leaned his head back against the booth. Jesse was always treating him like a king, homemade food, thoughtful dates, acts of kindness, he had to think of something. He was quiet for a long time, chewing too many times on a French fry.

"How do you...I...we...ugh." Hunter knocked his elbows onto the table and buried his face in his hands.

"Spit it out man!" Shay laughed shaking his arms.

"What kind of present shows someone you care?... about them." Hunter said placing his intonation on the wrong parts of the sentence.

"Are you saying what I think you're saying?" Shay gasped dramatically, her eyes lighting up. Hunter squeezed his eyes shut and tipped his head up to the ceiling.

"Mmkay no. No I am not."

"Cause I think you're saying you have feelings for—"

"Nope, no, no. I am saying it might be nice for me to thank him with a birthday...gift or like something." Hunter flipped his hands and Shay giggled at him, amused.

"Oh how sweet are you, saying thank you for sex." Shay shimmied her shoulders and smirked smugly.

"Oh my gosh why are you like this?" Hunter gesticulated cringing outwardly.

"Relax, I'm just fucking with you." Shay giggled, "Why don't you cook for him? He does that for you. Or surprise him with his favorite takeout meal?" Shay shrugged

"I can't cook and I don't know what his favorite food is." Hunter punctuated his words with his fingers on the table.

"You've been seeing him for four months and you don't know his favorite food?" She shook her head in disbelief

"Okay in my defense, he doesn't have a regular order from here. He changes it every single time he's here."

"Okay what about something totally out of the ordinary? I'll send you a list of places I like." Shay pulled out her phone and texted him. "I'll cover you here, go plan something special, really think Hunter, use your brain." Shay tugged the basket with the remaining fries closer to her and tossed a key from her pocket onto the table.

"What is this?" Hunter grimaced.

"The key to Jesse's place. I only have it for emergencies, but I think it'd be okay if I let you borrow it in exchange for these." She smiled snapping down on another fry.

"Thank you Shay." Hunter smiled pocketing the key. He kissed her cheek and grabbed his coat heading out the door.

Hunter drove around neighboring towns for the majority of the day, having borrowed his parents' car. He gathered what he thought was necessary, returned the car, and let himself into Jesse's condo. He worked methodically to set the table up, cartons of Thai food littering the table; noodles, pork buns, fried rice, shrimp rolls, spring rolls, and soup. Hunter slipped the thin box he had meticulously wrapped under the bench seat of the nook and boiled water on the stove for Thai tea. He poured the tea and added the milk and honey as the internet instructed him. As he placed the steaming mugs on the table he heard the telltale slide and click of a key in the door. Hunter felt his heart tick up a few notches in nervous anticipation. Jesse clicked the door closed behind himself and tugged the beanie off his head with a heavy sigh, in the same motion leaning his forearm against the closed door and pillowed his forehead against it.

"Surprise." Hunter said softly, leaned against the counter in the kitchen. Jesse jumped sky high and turned on his heel. He slammed his back against the door, hand to his chest.

"Shit Hunter." He gasped, feeling his heart speed in his chest, the wind knocked out of him.

"Sorry, sorry. Shay gave me your key and I know it's for emergencies, but she told me it's your birthday and I wanted to do something nice because I really am not quite good at that but I got us dinner and I scared the fuck out of you and I can just go if you want to be alone tonight." Hunter babbled out of nerves while Jesse tried to catch his breath. He shook his head and swiped at his forehead, still leaned against the door.

"I nearly gave you a heart attack." Hunter laughed lightly approaching him tentatively.

"You did." Jesse nodded seemingly frozen. Hunter danced his fingers on the shoulders of Jesse's coat, a smile teasing behind his eyes.

"Happy birthday." He whispered. A smile tugged at the corner of Jesse's lips and Hunter pulled him off the door, wrapping his long arms around Jesse's neck, pulling him in for a kiss. Their lips pressed together softly until Hunter dragged his tongue gently against Jesse's bottom lip as if asking permission, which he was granted. Jesse whimpered quietly, a soft desperate sound as his hand gripped the back of Hunter's neck, tilting his head at just the right angle to deepen their kiss. When they parted, their foreheads stayed connected. They breathed harshly against each other's mouths, silent for a long moment.

"You have no idea...how badly I needed that." Jesse whispered. Hunter pulled him closer, arms around his neck in a hug. There was something in those words, in the way Jesse sighed against his neck, that told Hunter to hug him tighter. He suddenly felt the urge to protect this person in his arms, to show Jesse what he felt without saying it.

"You want some dinner?" Hunter whispered, pressing a kiss to Jesse's temple just before he nodded. Hunter slid back from him pulling off his coat gently and hung it on the designated hooks. Jesse kicked off his boots and toyed with the hem of his heavy sweater, debating if it was comfortable or suffocating.

"Go change, get comfortable. I can reheat everything." Hunter smiled trotting off to the kitchen while Jesse went to the bedroom. He decided on a quick shower and exchanged his clothes for black joggers and a light blue cotton long sleeve. With curls still damp, Jesse joined Hunter in the kitchen in a quick twenty minutes, sliding into the nook with a quiet thanks.

"So I realized today that I do not have a clue what your favorite food is because you always order something different, so I decided to try something different. Shay recommended this Thai place and I just got a whole bunch of things for us to try, also this Thai tea that I read is good and you like tea so I—" Hunter's ramble was cut short by a press of Jesse's lips to his.

"This is perfect. Thank you." Jesse smiled as a blush spread from the apples of Hunter's cheeks to the tips of his ears.

"I can't believe you worked on your birthday." Hunter spoke around a mouthful of shrimp roll, both of their plates full to the brim.

"What else would I do?" Jesse shrugged, "Being on the water is calming, gives me something to focus my energy on. So I worked and I went to the cemetery to see my parents."

"Oh." Hunter breathed, subconsciously sliding closer to Jesse on the bench of the nook. His uncharacteristic need for closeness clicking in place in Hunter's head.

"Yeah." Jesse sighed twirling noodles around his fork. "I'm sorry I didn't tell you about today, what I was doing. I know the note was vague I just…have spent my birthday alone since they passed and I wasn't sure what kind of mood I would be in so…" Jesse trailed off shoveling the forkful of noodles in his mouth. Hunter rested a heavy hand on Jesse's thigh, pressed against his own under the table.

"You don't owe me an explanation. I hope I didn't over-step, I just…you deserve a good birthday." Hunter squeezed his thigh gently before pulling his hand back up to cut a dumpling on his plate. Jesse bit back a whine at the loss of contact, quickly pulling himself back together.

"I am now, thanks to you." Jesse smiled. There were no leftovers to be packaged, takeout containers and mugs drained. Hunter got up and cleared the table insisting that Jesse sit and relax. Hunter washed the dishes, talking through his day at the restaurant up to when he left. He joined Jesse at the table after pulling a pecan pie from the oven. Jesse's eyes widened and he hummed happily.

"I noticed you really enjoyed my mom's pecan pie on Christmas, so I asked her to teach me to make it for you."

Hunter served them each a slice. Jesse leaned back in the bench when his second slice of pie was done, fork clanking onto the empty plate.

"I'm glad you made me change. Sweatpants are the only option right now." Jesse smiled patting his full stomach. "I can't remember the last time I ate this much in one sitting." Jesse laughed lightly. After a day of feeling isolated and anxious, flooded with emotions that threatened to push him over the edge, Jesse did not imagine ending his birthday so happy, so truly content and grateful.

"There's one more thing." Hunter smiled tentatively.

"Hunter, I really do not think I can fit one more bite." Hunter reached under the bench and pulled out the thin box, about the size of a sheet of paper, he had placed there earlier. The matte navy blue wrapping paper was neatly creased and tied up with a grey ribbon and matching bow. Jesse's mouth hung open unattractively, his brain seemingly offline.

"It's just a little something." Hunter bit his lip nervously. What he didn't know was that Jesse hadn't received a gift of any sort in years. It took him a moment to make his hands move, untying the ribbon carefully and pulling the paper apart at the creases, in awe of the symmetry of it. Jesse opened the white box to find a packet of papers inside. Jesse's eyebrows knit in confusion.

"I got you pre-approved to adopt a pet." Hunter smiled. "I think a dog would make good company for you. I'm not sure what breed you would want or whatever, so I just got you set to go. You can pick out any one you want. And the gift card for Pat's Pets," Hunter outwardly cringed at the name, "can be used for any pet supplies. So if you really hate the idea of a dog or a cat, they sell fish you can use the gift card for." Jesse hadn't noticed the gift card at first. He was so shocked, he didn't say a word, flipping through the pages as his mind wandered. He had always wanted a dog, just was too busy to act on it since moving back to Peggy's Cove.

"Do you hate it?" Hunter grimaced and Jesse shook his head, a smile blooming on his lips.

"This is amazing. It's so…thoughtful. Can we go right now?" Jesse asked with an eager bounce. Hunter smiled fondly and shook his head. Jesse had said *we*. Hunter wasn't sure he truly meant it but he was hanging on to the word like a prayer.

"I think they're closed by eleven at night."

Jesse smiled in return and pulled Hunter in for a bruising kiss.

"Come to bed with me." Jesse's voice was low, eyes burning with desire. They clasped hands and slid out from the bench together, Hunter's eyes crinkling with the strength of his smile. He couldn't remember ever smiling that hard, yet he never had such a reason. Hunter kissed Jesse to the bedroom shoving him gently by the shoulders onto the soft mattress. Hunter crawled on top of him, refusing to break their kiss as they made their way up the bed.

"Let me take care of you tonight." Hunter whispered huskily into Jesse's ear, biting gently at his earlobe. Jesse's soft moan morphed into a groan as Hunter's body settled on his full stomach. Both men let out a quiet laugh, their kiss becoming a clash of teeth until Hunter began sucking a mark on Jesse's collarbone. Hunter spoke into the skin of his neck, "Happy birthday Jess." By far, this had been the best birthday Jesse had ever had.

Over the next week, they made small changes in Jesse's condo to accommodate a dog. Despite his excitement about potentially becoming a "we", Hunter insisted Jesse go find his dog on his own. He cited the importance of forming a deep bond and loyal connection with his new pet. Hunter buzzed around the restaurant, a ball of anxious excitement, all day.

"Hunter, you've brought table seven their order twice and gave the man at nine three glasses of water. Is everything okay?" Katie asked him as he punched an order into the computer. He sighed heavily, trying to bite back a smile.

"Jesse is getting a dog today. I just really want it to go well and he hasn't answered any of my texts." Hunter was practically vibrating as he spoke. Katie placed a hand on his shoulder matching his smile.

"So go wait for him. It's slow today."

"And do what? Wait on his doorstep carving a path up and down the walkway?" Hunter bounced his leg balancing on the ball of one foot.

"Good point. Bring fries to table twelve and ask him for a key later." Katie winked at him before slipping back into the kitchen. Hunter finished his paperwork in record time after closing and just as he finished his shift, his cell phone buzzed in his pocket. Hunter yanked it out, pressing it quickly to his ear.

"Hello?" He tried to school his voice to sound less hysterical.

"Hunter, come over when you're finished at work, I've got someone for you to meet." Hunter could hear the smile in Jesse's voice.

"I'm done! I'll be there in five." Hunter pumped his fist in the air victoriously and pulled his coat on as fast as he could. He made sure to lock up before walking over to Jesse's.

He knocked on the door giving a valiant effort at keeping his composure. Jesse let him in, greeting him with a casual kiss and grabbed his hand practically dragging him to the large dog bed nestled in the corner of the living room. A small, fluffy, black and sable puppy lay curled in a ball, sound asleep, taking up next to no space at all in the bed.

"She's a German Shepard." Jesse smiled proudly.

"Huge paws, she'll be a big one." Hunter squatted down scratching behind the puppy's one floppy ear. "What's her name?"

"Magnolia, Maggie for short. For my dad's ship, S.S. Magnolia." Jesse sat on the couch and leaned over the arm to see the puppy better. She yawned as she woke and rolled onto her back so Hunter could pet her belly.

"Easy choice?" Hunter smiled as the puppy tilted her head back and forth looking at Jesse upside down while Hunter scratched her belly.

"She chose me." Jesse shrugged. "I picked up Chinese on the way back." They both stood and walked to the kitchen, Maggie right on their heels pouncing on their feet as they walked. Jesse fed her dry puppy food, which she gladly devoured while they sat at the nook to eat. After dinner they sat on the couch, side by side, Maggie draped across both of their laps, front and back legs outstretched. Hunter scratched down Maggie's back, laying against the crook of Jesse's shoulder, Jesse's arm slung around his back. Maggie rested her chin on Jesse's thigh as he carded through her fur.

"You're thinking too loud." Jesse pressed a kiss to Hunter's forehead and paused the movie.

"Sorry." He mumbled hiding his smile in Jesse's shoulder.

"Don't apologize. What's on your mind?" Jesse asked scratching his blunt nails lightly on the back of Hunter's neck.

"This is…nice?" Hunter bit his lip and nuzzled into Jesse's neck. "I like it." He whispered. It felt very domestic and comfortable. The crook of his shoulder was Hunter's favorite spot, he was starting to believe it was made just for him.

"I like it too." Jesse smiled dipping his head to kiss Hunter. They settled back in and Jesse pressed play. Hunter wrapped his arms loosely around Jesse's waist as Maggie curled up in Jesse's lap. That night they slept with Maggie stretched out at the foot of the bed. Everything Hunter never knew he wanted was right there in bed with him.

Hunter flew through the doors of the cafe for his lunch with Shay. He leaned against the table of their regular booth, hands splayed on the Formica, out of breath.

"Whoa there buddy, take it easy." Shay smirked teasing him.

"I have to talk to you. Now." Hunter said between gasps of air.

"Here?" Shay looked around, he was drawing attention to them. Hunter shook his head. Shay grabbed their coffees and hooked his arm walking out the door. March brought along a crisp breeze and most of the last snowfall had melted away. Though Hunter still wore his winter ensemble, the locals shed their snow coats for something lighter, Shay included.

"So what's got you all worked up?" She asked when they were a safe distance from the cafe and Hunter's breathing had calmed.

"I got an email from an artist in New York today with an offer for a contract." Hunter began and Shay looked up at him giving him her attention. "Apparently he signed on with a planner that hasn't done a great job executing his vision." Hunter rolled his eyes, "Anyway, he'd like me to take over the contract for the rest of the year. It would be nine months of shows with ten percent commission on each piece sold and an incredible budget."

"That's amazing Hunter. Congratulations! When do you start?" Shay squeezed his arm tight.

"Never." He bit his lip gently as Shay pulled them both to a stop.

"What'd you mean? Isn't that a huge opportunity?" She scrunched her eyebrows together and turned to face him, unlinking their arms.

"It is, but I don't want to go back to New York." Hunter spoke slowly, his lips pursing, biting the inside of his cheek to stop himself from grinning.

"What?" Shay smiled brightly up at him. "Are you saying what I think you're saying?" She was practically bouncing on her toes.

"I want to stay in Peggy's Cove." Hunter nodded and Shay launched herself into his arms.

"You won't regret this Hunter." She mumbled into his sweater and he laughed lightly, hugging her tight.

"I know I won't."

"Have you told Jesse yet? Your family? We have to celebrate!" Shay pulled back holding his arms.

"Slow down, no. I have not told anyone yet. I'm going to Jesse's tonight to tell him, then I'll tell my family tomorrow." He pulled his lips between his teeth, quelling his excitement.

"I'm so fucking happy for you." Shay hugged him again. He was so grateful to have her, to know she would be happy if he stayed. The email was a wakeup call for him that he never wanted his lonely New York life back again.

Hunter made two stops before he stood at Jesse's door, arms full, knocking with his foot against the door. Jesse opened the door to a smiley Hunter, balancing two pizza boxes on one hand, holding a bouquet of creamy white flowers mixed in with long vines and large green leaves.

"Hi" Hunter breathed out. He walked into the condo pressing a kiss to Jesse's cheek and handed him the bouquet simultaneously.

"Hi, um these…for me?" Jesse stuttered looking over the stunning floral arrangement.

"Mmhmm, they're magnolias." Hunter smiled toeing off his shoes and pulled Jesse in for a proper kiss. Jesse's blush crept down his neck, Hunter imagined the effect it had on his muscled chest.

"I've never…no one's ever given me flowers." Jesse smiled latching onto the soft spot below Hunter's ear.

"Mm well if I knew you'd like them this much, I'd have done it months ago." Hunter smirked as Jesse slid his hands under the hem of Hunter's thick sweater, pulling his undershirt untucked from his jeans.

"And you brought dinner." Jesse growled softly in his ear.

"Dinner that I'm about to drop." Hunter laughed breathily as Jesse gripped his hip, thumb digging in above his hipbone.

"Okay, let's put this on pause. Get those in a vase and I will meet you in the shower." Hunter wiggled his eyebrows.

He tossed the pizza boxes in the oven on warm and quickly set up the bathroom. Jesse found a vase, filled it with water and gently dropped the bouquet in before following Hunter into the bathroom.

Hunter settled in on the bench of the nook, loose joggers and one of Jesse's sweatshirts wrapping him in warmth. He had towel dried his hair as best as he could until his stomach opposed, demanding dinner. Jesse slid on the bench beside him wrapping an arm around Hunter's shoulders, his boneless body limp against Jesse's shoulder. Jesse's sleep pants and white tee shirt hung loosely on his body and Hunter loved the feel of the worn cotton tee against his cheek.

"I'm bringing you flowers every day." Hunter smiled, completely blissed out, looking up at Jesse with half lidded eyes and blown pupils.

"I wouldn't object to that." Jesse smiled kissing Hunter in a gentle clash of teeth until his stomach interrupted them. "Let's get some food in you." Jesse rubbed his bicep nudging him up to a seated position on the bench. The boxes held two cheese calzones and a large pepperoni pizza.

After his first slice was gone, Hunter finally worked up the courage to speak.

"I have something to tell you." He smiled shyly picking pepperoni off his pizza.

"I actually have something to tell you too." Jesse smiled cutting a calzone in half, serving each of them a piece.

"You first." Hunter smiled crookedly, eating the displaced slice of pepperoni.

"Okay, so I was asked to go out on a week-long deep sea fishing trip to help bring in some money for the town." Jesse began.

"Oh?" Hunter asked prompting him to continue.

"Yeah. They wanted me to go next week, but I asked them to push it off until you go back home. I just feel like we've worked so hard training Maggie and I don't want to lose momentum with that. So I'll ask Shay to watch her while I'm gone." He shrugged and Hunter sputtered, nearly choking on a bite of pizza.

"After I go...home?" Hunter felt the color drain from his face.

"Yeah, the big city's waiting for you right? Just a month left 'til you're free to be you." Jesse smiled supportively. "So what's your news?" Hunter froze at the question. His mind was racing, the voice in his head telling him he was wrong to want to stay, wrong to want to be away from New York. Jesse wanted him to go, was waiting for the day he left to start his life again. His heart began to pick up speed.

"Hunter?" Jesse placed a hand on his thigh, the touch pulling him from his spiral.

"Yeah." Hunter whispered, not trusting his voice to be any louder.

"What did you want to tell me?" Jesse smiled fondly at him, giving his leg a squeeze.

"Oh um." Hunter paused, closing his eyes to regroup his thoughts. "I uh...I was offered a nine months contract with an artist in New York." He spoke quietly, his words slowly leaving his mouth without his permission.

"That's fantastic! New York is lucky to get you back." Jesse smiled and Hunter nodded silently. He played with the pizza left on his plate, ripping it apart gently and forked all the cheese from his half of calzone. Jesse wrapped their leftovers and cleared when they were finished.

"You okay? You usually peel off pizza." Jesse noted as he scraped Hunter's unfinished dinner into the trashcan.

"Mmhmm, not feeling well." Hunter said quietly, it wasn't a lie.

"Why don't you go wash up for bed, I'll take care of all this." Jesse kissed his forehead and busied himself with washing the dishes. Hunter trudged to the bathroom feeling like dead weight. He half-heartedly washed up and brushed his teeth before curling up on his side in the bed. How could he have misread the signs? He was so angry with himself for believing he could have this permanently, he should have known better. Hunter pretended he was asleep when Jesse climbed into bed behind him, wrapping his strong arms around Hunter's torso. Jesse slid a hand up his own sweatshirt that was on Hunter's body, resting against Hunter's soft lower belly. Hunter closed his eyes willing himself to disappear from his living nightmare.

Sleep evaded him, as he expected, so he gave up by two in the morning. He sat on the living room couch, Maggie in his lap and wrote a note to Jesse.

> Jesse,
> These past five months have been the best of my life, and I have you to thank for

that. You have so much ahead of you. Good
luck with Maggie.

Hunter

He gave a heavy sigh and leaned the note against the teapot on the counter. Hunter grabbed his overnight bag, pulled on his coat and shoes, and pulled the door closed quietly behind himself.

Jesse stalked into the restaurant early the next morning, note crunched in his fist as he approached the bar.

"Where's Hunter?" His voice broke, breathing hard. Katie looked up at him with red-rimmed eyes.

"He's gone." She said softly.

"Wha-what'd you mean gone where?" He asked, panic rising in his chest.

"New York." Katie looked at him with sympathetic eyes and Jesse took a step back shaking his head.

"No, he wouldn't."

"He has before, I should've seen this coming." Katie buried her face in her hands on the bar top. Jesse stumbled backwards over the leg of a bar stool and left the restaurant in a huff. Katie slammed her fist on the counter and pulled out her phone re-reading the text once again.

I have to go back to NY. Please call me.

She deleted the text and shoved the phone back in her pocket swiping surreptitiously at a tear that had escaped.

Hunter paced the gate at the airport early that morning. As much as he didn't want to leave, he didn't want to be where he was unwanted. Running a frustrated hand through his hair, he pulled his phone from his pocket and called his mom. He wanted to explain before she found he had left. It rang three times and just as he resigned to formulating a voicemail, she picked up.

"Hello?" Beth's voice was thick with sleep.

"Mom, I didn't mean to wake you." Hunter sighed heavily.

"Honey, is everything okay?" Worry etched itself in her voice, as any mid sleep phone call would cause a mother.

"I have to go back to New York. I'm sorry. I just couldn't see you...say goodbye" he sucked in a breath, keeping himself in check. This is why he could not face anyone. He was terrible at goodbyes.

"Hunter, we all knew this was the end goal. We have loved having you, but you're meant to be in New York, you always have. We're lucky to have had the time we did with you." Beth spoke softly.

"I know but...but maybe I *wanted* to stay." Hunter jammed his eyes shut at his admittance.

"Honey then—"

"I have to go mom, my plane is boarding." He sighed heavily, gathering his belongings as the last call was made.

"Okay sweet heart, call me when you land?" She asked.

"Mmhmm bye mom." Hunter whispered and hung up to board his flight.

Hunter was drained by the time he set his one bag down in his apartment. He was hasty to leave and decided to forego his bags and the clothes he had had kept at his parent's house in favor of getting the hell out of there as fast as he could. He ordered too much Chinese food from his favorite hole in the wall place in and took a steaming shower to scrub off the day. Clad in joggers and a tee shirt, he flopped onto his soft black couch. He had texted his mom when he landed but found himself wanting to speak to her again.

"Hello?" Beth answered cheerfully.

"Hi mom, sorry I had to hang up so fast earlier."

"You didn't have to call back sweetie."

"I know, I wanted to." He said airily. The bell rang and he buzzed his delivery up. Tipping the man, he took his food, sat cross-legged on the couch and put the phone on speaker.

"Honey, you can come back and visit whenever you'd like. You will always have a place here, this is your home too." Beth had thought about what Hunter had said, he wanted to stay. She knew what he needed to hear, that he was wanted.

"Thanks mom." Hunter swallowed around the lump in his throat. He heard Katie's voice in the background. "Mom, can I talk to Katie please." He heard his mom move the phone away.

"Katie, Hunter wants to speak to you." He heard Beth say to her.

"You can tell him, I never want to speak to him again."
Katie snapped and slammed the door shut.

"She's out right now sweetie." Beth lied.

"Mmhmm." Hunter hummed and sniffled quietly.

"Honey, she'll come around."

"She shouldn't. I made so many mistakes mom, why
can't I do anything right?" Hunter swiped at his eyes and
shoved a dumpling in his mouth hoping to push the emotion
away.

"We all handle challenges in our own way. You just have
a different path than others honey, doesn't mean it's wrong."
She sighed deciding it was best to change the subject. "When
can you come back?"

"I have a big contract, monthly events through the rest
of the year." Disappointment was evident in his voice.

"Christmas then?" She asked.

"Mm, the last event is December tenth, I should super-
vise breakdown and I can be on a plane the twelfth. That's
long but I'd like to stay through the New Year?" He asked
hesitantly, flipping through his calendar.

"We would love that. We'll count down the months and
it will just fly by." She tried to keep excitement in her voice.

"Thank you mom. I love you." Hunter whispered.

"I love you more baby. Take care of yourself okay?" She
asked and he hummed in response before ending the call.
Hunter scrubbed his hands over his face. Before he knew it,
the cartons all lay empty in his lap. The silence of his apartment was deafening, nothing to stop his racing thoughts. He
felt a panic attack coming on swiftly and made his way to
the bathroom hoping another shower would calm his nerves.
Opening the cabinet for a fresh bar of soap, he spotted a

small orange bottle. His hands acted before his weak mind could stop him, old habits die hard.

Katie buried her face in her scarf the second she shut the door and screamed as loud as she could into the soft material, successfully muffling the sound. She tied the scarf around her neck and took off for the docks. She spotted Jesse, perched on the rocks beside the lighthouse. She slid down beside him and wrapped him in a hug.

"He left a note." Jesse said staring out at the horizon.

"Any explanation?" Katie asked.

Jesse shook his head, "No. I would be less confused if he left without a trace." He laughed humorlessly.

"He called. Spoke to my mom on the phone." Katie spoke softly, sniffling and Jesse glanced at her expectantly. "I told her I didn't want to speak to him and I didn't stick around to hear what he had to say." Jesse nodded, he understood why she made her decision, but he couldn't help but wonder what Hunter would have said. Shay joined them then, having been notified of the time and place from Katie, pizza box in hand.

"I need a catch up, spark notes version preferred." Shay sat on Jesse's other side and balanced the box on a flat rock in front of them, grabbing a slice from the pie.

"Hunter's gone back to New York." Katie spoke with distaste on her tongue.

"Haa?" Shay asked around the pizza in her mouth.

"He up-and-left in the middle of the night. Jess woke up to a goodbye note." Katie clarified.

"Um why would he do that?" Shay shook her head in disbelief; this was certainly not what she imagined after what Hunter had told her yesterday. "Did something happen Jesse?"

"Last night," Jesse sighed shaking his head, "was incredible." He couldn't curb the smile that bloomed at the memory. "He brought me flowers and dinner. He was very, into it all. We both shared some big news and fell asleep. It felt…I dunno…right? It was comfortable and—"

"News? Jesse what news?" Shay asked feeling on edge.

"I'm going on a fishing trip and he had a job offer in New York." Jesse shrugged worrying his bottom lip. "I knew it wasn't serious, I just thought I'd get more than a fucking confusing note when he left. I thought I meant a little more than that to him." He looked down at his lap, tugging on a loose thread on the seam of his jeans.

"You really had feelings for him." Katie looked at him with wide eyes, her breath caught in her chest.

"It's fine, I'm used to people leaving." He mumbled, swallowing hard. He couldn't help the journey his mind was taking him on. His father had left him without a goodbye, his mother had left him without a goodbye and now, the person he thought cared for him enough to at least wave him off had also left without a goodbye. He feared he would never be enough for someone to find him worthy, for someone to stay.

"I'm sorry Jess." Katie pulled him in for a hug that he returned with desperation. He found himself in a place he promised he would never let himself get to again. The day his mother had taken her life, he felt more alone than he ever had before. She had left him, walked right out of his life. He was not enough for her to stay. He promised never to let anyone in enough to do the same, yet there he was. He clutched on to Katie, refusing to cry, that was not who he was. Jesse had been through a lot but he was strong as hell. He swallowed down the threatening emotion as Shay sat silently beside them, trying to piece together what had happened between her conversation with Hunter and his decision to leave.

Shay waited a few days to see if he would reach out. As expected, he graced her with radio silence. She called four days after he had left. She was not expecting him to answer so it surprised her when he picked up before the second ring.

"Shay" Hunter breathed her name into the speaker.

"What the fuck Hunter?" Shay was beyond taking his shit. She was angry, hurt and disappointed. She deserved some answers.

"I couldn't do it Shay." He let out a harsh breath.

"What happened? You were so sure, I just don't get it." Her voice softened, hearing the distress on his end of the phone.

"He didn't want me there." Hunter began speaking, his voice cracking.

"Hunter you—"

"Let me finish." He raised his voice desperately and Shay went silent. "He's going on some fishing thing for a week. He pushed it back so we could train Maggie better before I left, because he wanted her to have stability. He said the city is my home. He said I would be free when I left. He meant he would be free too." Hunter snatched the small round bottle from the counter, rolling the smooth plastic in his hand.

"You're coming to a very drastic conclusion." Shay tried to reason with him.

"Shay, you didn't see his face. His life was on hold, because of me. He's been wasting time with me when there's a world of possibilities out there for him. I was holding him back and I couldn't do that, not to someone I care for, not to him." Hunter let out a heavy breath, willing himself to check his emotions. He quietly opened the orange pill bottle to let himself float away.

"Hunter, I think that you guys just weren't communicating and you have to…" Shay was cut off by a shaky breath on the other line.

"I don't '*have to*' anything. Not anymore. I can't Shay, it's too much." Hunter had given up hope, she could hear it in his voice. He was tired, sad, and just done.

"Okay, alright. Just know that this hasn't been easy for him, or any of us. We miss you Hunter. I miss you." Shay declared.

"I'll call you soon okay?" Hunter uttered quietly.

"You better." Shay smirked. Hunter ended the call and slid down the wall of the bathroom. He had fucked it up big time now, but Shay wanted to stay in touch with him and that was more comfort than he knew he deserved.

Over the months that followed, Hunter spoke to his mom more than he had ever before. She had become his rock, his confidante. He called every day on his walk home from work regaling her with tales of fancy parties, peculiar artists, and difficult clients. He made time to call Shay weekly, appreciating how she kept him up on the town and its inhabitants. Periodic letters were hand written and mailed to Katie.

He hoped, to no avail, for a response, any type of contact from her. He had routines established, took on enough private clients to fill his days, but his life in the big city remained unsatisfying.

By August, he was already more than tired of the heat and humidity, his body longing for the chill of Peggy's Cove that once churned his stomach. His morning had begun awfully, he got rained on while walking to work, dropped his coffee on his shoes, accidentally deleted an important file he then spent hours trying to recover, mercifully, with success, and had to talk a client out of breaking their contract with the museum due to a poorly executed menu at their last event. He decided it would be in everyone's best interest for him to get a late lunch, pop a pill and wrap up early for the day. He picked up a bacon, egg and cheese sandwich on an everything bagel after logging off from the office. He found himself unable to wait until he got home, devouring it as he walked back to his apartment. His phone rang with an unknown number. While he wanted to ignore it, he was technically still on the clock and his calls were linked to his cell phone. He dropped the remaining piece of his sandwich back into the paper bag he was carrying, wiped his hands on a napkin and picked up his phone.

"Hunter Davis how can I help you?" He plastered on his customer service voice, complete with an exaggerated smile.

"Mr. Davis? My name is Connie. I have you as the emergency contact for Jesse Fischer. There's been an accident." The kind, even voice on the other line spoke quickly. Hunter felt his heart drop and his stomach flip. He froze on the spot, mid stride on a busy city sidewalk.

"Um what?" He shook his head, unable to process what he had just been told.

"He is being transported to Nova Scotia Hospital in Dartmouth." She said after repeating her initial message.

"O-okay." Hunter hung up in a daze, he felt dizzy and nauseous and he was pretty positive it wasn't the pill he had just taken. He took a minute to catch his breath and make his feet move in a forward progression once again. Once motion began, he took off at a run for his apartment, bagel forgotten. He called in a favor as he ran home and booked himself on the very next flight to Halifax. He shoved a few essentials in his overnight bag, stuck his laptop in it's travel case, and hailed a cab to the airport. He tried calling his family, tried Shay, no one answered and he was at a loss for what to say in a voicemail. Hunter walked through the airport in a daze. As he boarded the plane, he realized he had no idea what he would find when he landed. Questions buzzed through his head; Did Jesse even care about him? Was Jesse even alive? How had he let things get this far? His fall from grace seemed to happen all at once and the guilt of leaving Jesse without closure began to consume him. He took two more pills from his unmarked travel case as they hit cruising altitude, an hour before landing. He hadn't felt this desperate and out of control since prior to his trip to Peggy's Cove. It was unsettling. He had to do something to calm himself before he arrived. After the most anxious flight Hunter had ever taken, he darted out of the airport and hailed a cab to the hospital. Hunter gave his information at the security desk and was directed up to a small waiting room on the eighth floor. The moment he turned the corner, he felt the air leave his lungs. Spread out in the chairs around the waiting room he saw his parents, Katie, and Shay along with a few others he recognized from the docks. Katie spotted him first and stood from her chair, crossing toward him.

"What are you doing here?" She nearly growled, anger dripping in her voice. Hunter sucked in a breath and met her half way, collapsing to his knees in front of her, wrapping his arms tight around her waist.

"I'm sorry. I'm so sorry." He mumbled through choked sobs, burying his face in her stomach. Katie stood dumbstruck for a moment before wrapping her arms around his shoulders. His body shook as he cried to her apologizing desperately, fists gripping her sweater with white knuckles. Katie took a breath to calm herself, letting her anger go for the sake of her brother.

"Okay, calm down. Come on, come let's go for a walk." She hooked her arms under his, practically dragging him to his feet. Looping their arms together, she walked him outside to the courtyard, the crisp, warm air surrounding them as they sat on a bench. Hunter swiped at his puffy, wet eyes with the sleeves of his sweatshirt, hiccupping staggered breaths.

"I'm sorry Katie." He mumbled and she hooked his arm again.

"Why did you go?" She asked looking up at him. Hunter took a steadying breath and launched into the story of the last night he had spent in Peggy's Cove with Jesse. By the time he finished, fresh tears were sliding down his cheeks.

"Why didn't you tell me?"

"I wanted to. I tried to call, I wrote to you." He sighed leaning on her shoulder.

"You promised you wouldn't give this up again, but you walked away." Katie rubbed his back. "He cares about you, you know. He had feelings for you."

"I couldn't hold him back. That wasn't fair." Hunter looked at her with red-rimmed eyes, desperate for her to understand.

"Did you ever think that that's why we didn't ask you to stay? We all love you so much we didn't want to hold you back from going for your dreams, from living the life you built for yourself." Katie reasoned with him.

"I guess that makes sense." Hunter shrugged covering his face with his hands, pulled into his sweatshirt. "I messed up Katie. I've screwed up." He bit his lip to swallow down a sob that tried to bubble its way out. Katie took his face in her hands and turned him to look at her. Hunter's half-lidded eyes were bloodshot and glassy, pupils blown, dark circles shadowing underneath.

"What'd you take?" She asked, eyes widening in recognition.

"Just tell me he'll be okay." He closed his eyes tight.

Katie sighed, "They think so, he's in surgery."

"What happened?" Hunter felt his guilt creep in again.

"Rough waters, one of the crew went overboard and Jesse jumped in after him. He took on water, hit his head pretty hard. He's in surgery for a broken leg. The captain that pulled him out gave him CPR, they think that's what broke his ribs." Katie explained carefully.

"This is my fault." Hunter shook his head.

"It is certainly not your fault. You're here now that's what matters." Katie stood offering her hand, "Let's go see if there's any news."

When they returned to the waiting room, Shay was alone.

"He's out of surgery, not awake yet though. Your parents are in with him. Everyone else went home." Shay pulled Hunter into a hug and she and Katie exchanged tentative smiles over his shoulder. Despite everything, they were glad to have him back. They settled in on the chairs again, Hunter's head in Katie's lap fighting off sleep as she fingered through his hair. He hadn't realized he drifted off until distant voices swam around his head, muffled and hard to make out.

"I want to get him home." Beth said to Katie after returning to the waiting room.

"He'll want to go see Jess first." Katie responded.

"He looks like he hasn't eaten a proper meal in days." Jack commented, glancing at his son's sunken-in cheeks.

"Wake him up, let him go in and I'll stay with Jesse for the rest of visiting hours." Shay offered. Random words penetrated his brain, but Hunter's head was foggy, unable to track the conversation. Then, he was being shaken into full wakefulness.

"Hunter come on, let's go see Jesse." Katie had pulled him to his feet and was dragging him down the hall.

"Are you going to be okay?" Katie stopped him outside the room. Hunter swallowed hard and shrugged.

"I don't really know." He said honestly, still feeling a bit hazy.

"I'll be right here with you." She squeezed his hand tight. Hunter tried to prepare himself. After what Katie had told him, he assumed Jesse would be worse for the wear. They both sat on Jesse's left in the two chairs left by their parents. Jesse's right leg was bandaged from mid-thigh down over his foot and raised up on a stack of pillows, his right arm was also wrapped, laying at his side. A long, angry looking laceration ran from his forehead, over his brow, and down to his cheekbone, stitched together with stark black thread. Underneath it all, Hunter could still see the Jesse he knew, soft, kind, understanding. He reached out and took his hand giving it a gentle squeeze, mindful of the IV taped to the back of his hand.

"You alright?" Katie asked quietly. He hadn't noticed the tears tracking down his face until she asked and he shook his head in response. She wrapped an arm around him, laying on his shoulder.

"He won't want to see me. I don't deserve his forgiveness." Hunter bit his lip hard.

"You don't know that, maybe you just need to give him some time." Katie assured him. Hunter pressed his lips to Jesse's palm, a warmth filling his chest for the first time since he left Peggy's Cove as a sob escaped him.

"Let's get you home." Katie said walking back to the waiting room with Hunter.

When they arrived home, Katie took Hunter upstairs. She insisted he shower and she tucked him into his bed when he was through. She didn't miss that he had pulled on a sweatshirt she recognized as Jesse's, the one he had taken when he left haphazardly in the middle of the night. Beth made egg drop soup and baked chicken sandwiches, which Hunter ate in bed. Katie never left his side and he felt like the world was wrapping him up in a warm, soft blanket. He knew he had a long way to go, but this was as good a start as any.

The days passed in a blur for Hunter. He oscillated between nausea, sweats and chills in his minimal waking hours and forced himself to sleep off the effects of the drugs he pumped his body with. Hunter woke from a particularly long nap in a pool of his own sweat to the smell of chicken soup and the sound of his sister's voice.

"He's been out for hours." Katie spoke softly, dragging a hand through her hair before sweeping it up into a ponytail.

"He's been sleeping too much, I'm worried." Beth sighed pressing a hand to his forehead. The touch stung his prickling skin, but he was too drained to move away or protest, even his eyes hadn't yet received the memo that his brain was awake.

"It's only been a couple of days, Mom. He needs time. Trust me it's better he sleeps." Katie paused, "I'll make sure he eats." She continued. Hunter could only imagine the look his mother must have given her.

"My sweet boy." Beth sighed heavily. Even when he had returned, he was causing his mother distress, the one person he relied on during all those months alone in New York. "Tell Jess I said hi. I'll be there tomorrow for breakfast, get his order for me?" Katie asked and Hunter felt his heart clench and his stomach turn.

"Of course." Beth smiled closing the door behind her. Before he could even open his eyes, Hunter found himself leaned over the side of his bed emptying his stomach into the trash can that has become a staple. Katie tutted at him, rubbing his back and helped him settle back against his pillows. When she brushed his sweat soaked hair from his forehead he flinched away.

"Let's get you a shower." Katie decided, setting the bathroom up for him. She changed his sheets while he was showering and made him a fresh cup of tea. It wasn't long before Shay joined her, sitting beside her on the edge of Hunter's bed waiting for him to return.

"How is he?" Katie asked, concern in her tired eyes.

"He's tired, a little disoriented, still in a lot of pain. How's he?" She asked nodding her head toward the bathroom.

"He's slept a lot. Mom's worried, but I think he'll be okay." Katie nodded and Hunter entered the room wearing the pajamas Katie had left for him, his hair damp from the shower, smelling like his cedar wood cleanser. Hunter let himself flop onto the sheets from the foot of the bed, laying behind Katie and Shay.

"Do you want some soup?" Katie asked, turning to face him.

"Please no." Hunter begged, his eyes pleading with her, "The smell is killing me."

"You've got to eat something." Katie sighed, standing to open his window for some fresh air, "I'll go pick you up anything, just tell me what you want."

Hunter groaned in response and Shay shrugged, "What about a bagel? The café is open. I'll stay here." Shay offered, knowing Katie could use the break.

"Thanks, that's a good idea. Will you eat it?" Katie asked and Hunter nodded silently. Katie thanked Shay once more before leaving the two alone.

"How are you holding up?" Shay asked, turning to face him.

"Feel like shit." He mumbled and Shay chuckled in response. "Everything makes me nauseous and my skin hurts." Hunter grumbled, hauling himself to sit against his headboard. Shay nodded, giving him a once over. He looked thinner than she had last seen him, tired and worn in a way that showed how he wore his guilt. Hunter squirmed, uncomfortable under her gaze. "How's Jess?" He asked quietly.

"A little better than yesterday. He's sleeping a lot, pretty uncomfortable, but he's strong, he'll be okay." Shay twisted her fingers in her lap, staring down at them. "You should go see him." She wasn't sure it was her place, but she knew it had to be said.

"Has he asked for me?" Hunter asked, hope building inside him that he hadn't felt for months.

"He doesn't know you're here." Shay watched his shoulders drop.

"He needs to recover. He doesn't need me screwing something else up for him. Maybe it's best he doesn't know I'm here for now. He deserves to be able to decide if he sees me. I owe him that much." Hunter conceded and Shay nodded, though she didn't necessarily agree, she knew better than to argue with Hunter.

Three days had passed, before Jesse brought it up. He had spent most of his time sleeping, the pain medication taking its toll. Though he appreciated the company, Jesse was used to being alone, so the revolving door of visitors left him feeling suffocated.

"I know you're not asleep and I'm not leaving." Shay smirked knowingly. Jesse sighed, opening his eyes to glare at her. "I'm not here to bother you Jess, I have food." She tossed a grease stained brown paper bag onto his lap and reached for the controls at the side of his bed, tilting him up to a semi-seated position.

"I'll allow it." Jesse smiled, digging through the bag with one hand, his bandaged arm at his side.

"That arm's not broken, ya know." She reminded him and he glared at her once more.

"I am well aware, thank you. You try functioning with thirty stitches pulling at your arm." He countered and Shay grimaced.

"Alright, alright, I get it." She sat in the chair beside him as he ate the fish tacos and sweet potato fries she had brought him from Catch of the Day.

"I have something crazy to tell you." Jesse said handing her his empty cup of water and crumbled brown bag.

"What is it?" Shay asked, tossing it in the trash. She leaned back in her chair and crossed her feet where they were perched on his bed, adjacent to his knees.

"I had a dream I think…that Hunter was here." He said tentatively. Shay sighed meeting his eyes.

"Go on." She prompted.

"I don't know why. I haven't really thought about him in months. It seemed so real though, felt like he was here. It's stupid." He sighed flipping his hand as if to fling the thought away.

"Jesse, it isn't stupid. He uh…he was here. Your dispatcher called him, your emergency contact." She paused and raised her eyebrows. "He came back, but he wasn't sure you would want to see him."

"Huh." Jesse huffed and closed his eyes.

"You've gone through a lot. It's important you rest and keep the stress to a minimum." Shay gave him an out.

"I…why'd he come then?"

"You're going to have to ask him, when you're ready." She shrugged.

"Bring him here?" Jesse asked, eyes pleading.

"Are you sure?" Shay was uncertain.

"Please" He whispered, closing his eyes against the harsh light.

Shay brought Hunter the next day, as promised, with Katie in tow. Hunter had kept his anxiety at bay, but felt it rush him like a linebacker as he approached Jesse's room. Katie had agreed to wait in the hall while Shay accompanied him. When they walked in Hunter didn't notice anything different except that Jesse was awake and sitting mostly upright. Hunter gave a short wave as Shay dragged him to one of the chairs beside the bed.

"Hi." Jesse spoke first, clenching his fist around the sheets.

"How are you?" Hunter bit his lip, regretting the question immediately.

"Been better." Jesse shrugged, lips pulled to a slight smirk.

"I...yeah. No, I know that." Hunter sighed heavily, staring at a hole in the sheets. Eye contact was not an option. "I have to explain." He started, pausing for a breath.

"No you don't." Jesse shrugged. "You don't *have* to do anything." Bitterness seeped into his words, surprising even Jesse, himself.

"I-I want to. I was wrong to leave the way I did. I liked you...like you a lot. It scared me because I knew I was expected to go back and not have feelings for you. I was afraid I was holding you back from your life and you never asked me to stay or told me you wanted me to, which I know now was unfair to put on you." Hunter rushed out in one breath. "I guess I just want to say I'm sorry."

"Is that all you came for? To clear your conscience?" Jesse felt the bite his words held, knowing they would hit Hunter where it hurt and watched him flinch with the sting.

"No, of course not." Hunter sighed, "When I got that phone call it all came flooding back to me, every feeling I had for you that I tried to push away and bury, like I'd never left."

138

"How long are you here?" Jesse asked.

"I'm done with New York. I want to stay." Hunter glanced at him quickly, wanting Jesse to know he meant it.

Jesse let out a heavy breath, exhaustion clear on his face. "It took me a long time to get over you." He admitted, his voice growing thick with fatigue and the emotion that threatened to bubble over. "I appreciate your apology, but I'm not sure I'm ready to do anything about it...just yet." Hunter nodded in understanding. "I have a pretty extensive undertaking to deal with here. Just, I think I need time."

"Of course, I will be here. Whenever you're ready to talk." Hunter swallowed hard.

"I'll call you then." Jesse whispered and Hunter nodded, before excusing himself from the room. Shay gave Jesse a kiss on the cheek, following Hunter out.

Hunter didn't expect Jesse to just throw caution to the wind and go back to where they left off, he understood that he would have to work to regain his trust. The problem was, Jesse wasn't willing to let him in at all, he had dismissed Hunter keeping the ball in his own court. Hunter felt helpless, so he sunk into the restaurant day and night. He worked open to close every day with one of his parents. He refused a day off, even when his family insisted. It was a much needed distraction, something to keep his body and mind busy while he gave Jesse the time he had promised. Shay was taking care of Maggie and she and Katie took shifts with Jesse at the hospital, so he wouldn't be alone. He was set to come home on Monday, two weeks after the accident. Hunter's parents would be picking him up to drive him back to Peggy's Cove. The weekend was planned to a T, everyone pitching in to cook, clean, and make accommodations for Jesse's return. Hunter wanted to do something, he wracked his brain for something subtle and came up with, what he felt, was the perfect gesture. He gave Shay a fresh pecan pie and a vase of Magnolias with her promise to leave them in Jesse's condo. Sunday morning came with a rush of guests filling the restaurant. It was the busiest it had been since Hunter returned and he was grateful for the distraction. Shay popped in at the end of the breakfast rush to pick up a quick lunch.

"The town is crowded this weekend." Shay commented to Hunter, "I'm sold out."

"That's great Shay." Hunter smiled.

"Hey can you do me a favor?" She asked and Hunter hummed in acknowledgement. "I have so much to do, I hate to ask, but could you please feed Maggie tonight?"

"Shay, I—"

"He won't have to know. Please Hunter? Your mom and Katie are working triple time in the kitchen to stock his freezer and I have to drive to Halifax to fill his prescriptions and pick up bus tickets for a guest." Shay pleaded with him.

"Fine, fine." He sighed, "Give me the keys." Shay smiled tossing the keys on the counter and kissed his cheek, "Thank you so much! You're saving my ass here."

After locking up the restaurant, Hunter made the trek to Jesse's house in light summer rain. He wasn't used to walking Peggy's Cove in only a thin cotton Henley, though he was glad to get used to it. He stepped into Jesse's condo, instantly flooded with the memory of the last night he was there, one of the happiest moments of his life handing flowers to the man he was too afraid to admit he loved. Love, that was a brand new thought. He tugged off his shoes and was nearly plowed down by Maggie, who had grown three times her size in the six months of his absence.

"Whoa, you're huge! Hi girl, hi. I missed you." Hunter knelt down as she lapped up his face. He was glad her one ear had stayed floppy, it gave her character. When she finished her elaborate greeting, she barked loudly at him and ran to the bedroom.

"Come on, come get your dinner." He called as he poured the dry kibble into her bowl and refreshed her water. He could hear her whine from the bedroom, then she ran back to him, barked and disappeared again. Hunter patted his thighs and called out to her again. When she returned she bit onto his shirt and shook her head, nearly ripping holes into it.

"Easy Maggie, what's gotten into you?" He chastised her when she let go. She jumped up, her front paws nearly reaching his shoulders and barked again. He sighed in resignation and followed her to the bedroom when she retreated again.

"Oh my gosh." Hunter stumbled back, surprised to see Jesse on the floor, back against the bed, legs sprawled in front of him. His crutches just out of reach by the foot of the bed. Maggie sat down between Jesse's legs and whimpered.

"What are you doing here?" Jesse grumbled.

"What are *you* doing here?" Hunter shot back, too shocked to react any differently.

Jesse let out a tired sigh, "I got discharged a day early. Took a cab back to town." Hunter nodded his head four times in rapid succession.

"Mmhmm and how'd that work out for you?" Jesse shot him a look, his jaw clenching.

"Here." Hunter stepped closer offering a hand but Jesse held up his hand signaling to stop.

"No, I've got it." He said gripping his nightstand with one arm, his bandaged arm grabbing the bed. Hunter stood back as Jesse attempted to hoist himself up before hissing in pain, both arms curled around his ribs. Hunter stood his ground, fighting the urge to help. Instead, he lowered himself to the ground a few feet from Jesse and leaned against the foot of the bed. Maggie laid her head on Jesse's lap seemingly showing support. It took a few minutes for Jesse's breathing to come back down, though his face still wore a pained expression.

"What do you want?" He sighed defeated.

"To talk, will you listen?" Hunter folded his arms, knowing he had Jesse cornered he couldn't let this opportunity pass him by. Jesse nodded in response tipping his head back against the nightstand with a *thunk*. Hunter took a breath, he knew he'd been given a chance to make amends, what he'd been hoping for. In this room, in the dark, where he'd lost all his inhibitions and gained so much more. He was willing to risk it all to get back that feeling. If it didn't go his way, at least he would know he had tried.

"When I came here that night, I was planning to tell you that I turned down the job in New York, that I was staying. I'd told Shay earlier that was my plan." Hunter looked up, Jesse's eyes were closed but he was listening. "When you told me about your trip, I was afraid to disappoint you. You made plans around me leaving and I was having all these... these feelings. I was getting the impression that you didn't feel the same." Jesse picked his head up and glanced over at Hunter.

"What changed your mind?" He asked breathlessly.

"I got a phone call that you were in trouble, because I am your emergency contact." Hunter heard his own voice crack, swallowed and continued. "The second I knew I meant that much to you I was right back in it." They were surrounded in silence, both breathing heavy, nerves on edge. "Someone told me once, that mending the bridges you burned can be worth the work and the pain. I realized I'm willing to put in the work to fix this bridge, because it's the best damn bridge I've ever built, as unintentional as it was." Hunter's lip quirked up gently on one side.

"Yeah." Jesse said on an exhale, his vision blurred by tear-filled eyes.

"Maybe we can start with what happened here?" Hunter queried, raising an eyebrow.

"I was on my way back from the bathroom." Jesse stopped, gulping around the lump in his throat. He was embarrassed, he couldn't even get to and from the bathroom without help and the whole situation was making him emotional.

"Will you let me help you up?" Hunter asked and Jesse nodded, jamming his eyes shut. Hunter rose from the floor and propped the fallen crutches against the wall. He stood over Jesse, assessing him, calculating how to get him up without hurting him.

"I think I've got it. Bend your knee, foot flat on the ground." Hunter instructed. Jesse did as he was told, planting the foot of his uninjured leg on the floor. Hunter squatted next to him, pulled Jesse's arm around his own shoulders and used one foot in front of Jesse's to root it to the spot. Hunter hoisted Jesse to his feet, met with a painful groan as he sat him on the edge of the bed. Jesse laid his forehead against Hunter's chest, his breaths coming in shaky gasps. Hunter held the back of Jesse's head, stepping closer, between his knees. Jesse gripped the back of Hunter's shirt with one hand as Hunter rubbed his back.

"I've got you." Hunter assured him and Jesse finally let go, sobbing freely into Hunter's shirt.

"Please don't go." Jesse's voice sounded strained, helpless as his tears bled through Hunter's shirt.

"I'm not going anywhere." Hunter whispered cupping the back of his head, curling himself down to press a kiss to the mess of curls.

Once Jesse regained his composure, Hunter made sure to give him his pain medication. It took a bit to kick in, but soon he had Jesse leaning back against a cluster of pillows at his headboard. Hunter had brought him food from the fridge that his mom had made and walked back into the bedroom with a fresh travel mug of tea in his hands.

"I made chamomile with honey, hope that's okay." Hunter passed the tumbler over, straw sticking out the top.

"Thanks, perfect." Jesse slurred his words, a sleepy smile on his face.

"Okay, are you sure you were supposed to medicate again?" Hunter was mildly concerned, but couldn't help the smile that grew on his face.

"Mmhmm, feel good." Jesse wiggled around and grimaced as he pulled his ribs.

"You left me pretty flowers." Jesse smiled, showing more teeth than necessary.

"I did, I hoped you'd like them." Hunter smiled back at him.

"I do. Get me more flowers Hun'er." Jesse blinked up at him sheepishly.

"Mmkay sure. I have to go make some calls, you okay?" Hunter asked setting up Jesse's laptop to play a movie. Jesse nodded, sipping his tea quietly. Hunter stood up, brushing a stray curl from Jesse's forehead and pressed a gentle kiss right next to the stitched cut on his forehead. As he turned to leave the room, he felt Jesse's hand grip his wrist. He turned on his heel, surprised.

"I'm glad you came back." Jesse locked eyes with him, the same tired gaze, whiskey brown eyes that made Hunter stay inexplicably that first night they spent together stared back at him. The familiar tug that Hunter tried so desperately to shake away was a welcome feeling to him now and he smiled brightly, lacing his fingers with Jesses' and brought his hand up to place a kiss on his knuckles.

"I missed you too." Hunter dropped his hand gently to the bed, "Be back soon." He promised. After calling Shay and his parents to let them know where he was and that Jesse was home, Hunter went back to the bedroom. Jesse was sound asleep, tipped to the side, his lips parted slightly, Maggie curled beside his feet. Hunter bit back a smile and slid Jesse down the bed slowly by his hips, tucking him in gently. Hunter slid under the sheets and fell asleep with a smile on his face.

Jesse was home a week before his first follow up appointment. It had been an eventful week, company consistently coming and going from his small condo. Hunter started seeing a therapist ten minutes out of town, three times a week. Those became his days off from the restaurant and after his appointments, he would spend the day with Jesse. Shay drove Jesse back to the hospital for the removal of his stitches and staples. His leg was put in a hard cast to help him move easier with less pain. Hunter, predictably, was sour that he was unable to take Jesse, but he had insisted Hunter not break his therapy schedule. So instead, he resorted to texting Shay every few minutes for updates. She ignored him after the first hour, annoyed by his insistence. He was given the courtesy of one text after Shay had Jesse home and settled in bed.

Rough day. Your turn.

Hunter groaned responding that he'd tag her out in ten. He stopped to pick up the fries Jesse liked from the restaurant and let himself into the condo with the key that now held a permanent place on his own keyring.

"He's going to play it off like it's nothing, pain in the ass." Shay grumbled. "He can take pain meds in an hour, set an alarm so you don't forget." She grabbed a fry, popping it into her mouth, "I deserve this." She mumbled with her mouth full.

"Anything I need to know?" Hunter asked, tucking the bag away on the counter and out of her reach.

"Nothing life changing, cast can't get wet, that's important. There's some kind of scar treatment I put in the top drawer in the bathroom that should be used on his head and his arm twice a day. He can use the crutches but no weight bearing and be mindful of the ribs." She ticked off the list on her fingers as Hunter nodded along, a distant look in his eyes. "Hey, you okay?"

"Yeah, why wouldn't I be?" Hunter asked snapping his attention back to her.

"Well, after running away for six months you came back and got thrown to the sharks. Aside from work and therapy, which is enough in and of itself to be overwhelming, you're taking care of Jesse like it's your full time job." Shay folded her arms, she knew this would be a lot to balance on a good day, let alone after all Hunter had gone through.

"It's not, I couldn't even be there for him today." Hunter huffed a frustrated breath.

"You aren't expected to do it all, Hunter. Not by me or your family or Jesse. You need to put yourself first sometimes too, especially now. You've been so caught up with worrying about him," She sighed, "just don't forget to check in with yourself every once in a while."

"You sound like my therapist." Hunter rolled his eyes, but smiled fondly.

"Except I'm better." Shay smirked, stealing another fry before letting herself out. Hunter knocked on the bedroom door to find Jesse sat up in bed, navy blue plaster disappearing up under his basketball shorts.

"Look I'm mobile." Jesse smiled, though Hunter noticed it didn't reach his eyes. His voice sounded heavy, tired.

"That's great honey." Hunter smiled greeting him with a kiss and ran the pad of his thumb gently down the raised scar on his forehead, still pink but now free of stitches. "Less Frankenstein, more Harry Potter, I like it." Hunter pressed a kiss to the tender skin and Jesse hummed, eyes closed.

"This one's better too." He turned over his arm to show another thick, raised scar that stretched from elbow to wrist, no longer needing the bandage to cover it. Hunter took the bait and peppered light kisses down the scar.

"I brought you French fries." Hunter tossed the greasy bag onto Jesse's lap.

"Yes!" Jesse pumped his fist and tore open the bag.

"How was it today?" Hunter asked, settling next to Jesse as Maggie jumped up and flopped into Hunter's lap, rolling over for belly rubs.

"Fine." Jesse mumbled around a mouthful of potato.

"So was therapy." Hunter deadpanned and Jesse sighed.

"Okay, fine, it was great. I'd love to go back next week and have more staples yanked out of my skin." Jesse snarked and Hunter cringed. Jesse sighed heavily, "It actually wasn't as bad as I assumed. The cast hurt more surprisingly, guess having hardware for bones is not particularly comfortable. They said my ribs look okay? I dunno, they don't look okay, or feel okay to me but what do I know." Jesse pulled up his shirt showing Hunter the yellow and green bruise over his right side.

"Better than they were I guess?" Hunter shrugged.

"They said it could be six months before I get back to work. What the fuck am I gonna do for six months?" Jesse brought his fist down onto the cast in frustration.

"Me?" Hunter quipped with a sly smirk and a crimson blush unfurled from the apples of Jesse's cheeks down the collar of his shirt. "We'll figure something out. You can get around better now, maybe you can come hang at the restaurant? Or do something stationary down at the docks." Hunter's suggestion was met with a biter scoff.

"How was therapy?" Jesse asked, desperate to change the subject.

"Peachy, a very expensive hour's worth of reliving my misfortune at the hands of a city I gave everything to. So it turns out there's a bunch of emotional damage that I blamed myself for? And I *am* partially to blame." Hunter looked down at his lap as he spoke and Jesse took his hand, squeezing gently. "Um but then, my amazing boyfriend swooped in to save me." Hunter let out a breathy laugh, a smile blossoming on his face. "You taught me so much, showed me what it was supposed to be like in a relationship. You care for me and you put me first, you learned me. I felt like I owed you something, I still very much do. But I think I realize that that debt of gratitude isn't an I owe you, or a keeping score, it's because I love you." Hunter looked up when he heard Jesse's little gasp and squeezed his hand tight. "You don't have to—"

"Hunter, stop." Jesse let his hand go to cup his cheek gently. "I've known for a long time, but I didn't want to scare you off." He laughed lightly and Hunter smiled, tears filling his eyes. "I love you." Jesse smiled leaning in to capture Hunter's lips. Hunter tucked himself into the crook of Jesse's shoulder, sliding his hand up his thin tee shirt and spread his fingers out, palm flat on Jesse's stomach. Jesse chuckled lightly into the kiss and slung a strong arm around Hunter's shoulders pulling him flush against his own chest.

Physical therapy was physically exhausting for Jesse. For someone so active at work, especially with his arms, having been confined to a bed for nearly a month left him lethargic and stagnant. He had been excited to begin therapy, hoping for clearance to lift weights fairly quickly, but was disappointed to be achy and sore after his first session.

"I literally stretched and walked around on crutches. What is wrong with me?" Jesse roared, arms flailing and face red, from his spot on the couch. Hunter was reasonably concerned, Jesse had been so quiet on the drive home and the outburst came after he had helped Jesse to the couch and fetched him a bottle of water.

"Nothing's wrong with you." Hunter attempted to placate him, but didn't get far. Jesse crushed the drained water bottle and chucked it across the room where it bounced off the wall only to be retrieved by Maggie.

"I've reeled in a catch taller than myself, supported a crew of fifty, steered a ship through storms with forty mile an hour winds." Jesse's voice was loud, vexed, his face growing redder as he spoke. "Now look at me! I'm completely fucking useless."

"Okay, look at *me*." Hunter knelt in front of him, beside the couch and took Jesse's face in his hands. "You are not useless, you just feel that way because you can't work right now and you're a workhorse by nature. You will be able to do all those very intense things again someday, though I would much prefer you dock before storms going forward." Jesse huffed out a small laugh. Hunter rubbed the cool pads of his thumbs on the apples of Jesse's burning cheeks as he continued. "For now, we are going to forget about therapy because it's over and there's nothing we can do about it. I found my mom's lasagna in the freezer, so I am going to put that in the oven and, though I know you're not supposed to on your medicine, we are going to open a nice bottle of sweet red wine because *we* have had a terrible day." Jesse nodded worrying his lip and grabbed onto Hunter's wrists like a lifeline.

"I didn't realize you had a bad day too." He closed his eyes feeling guilty.

"Of course I did. My boyfriend is really struggling right now, I'm very shaken and I'm not sure I'm equipped to take care of him, but that is not going to stop me from trying." Hunter declared and Jesse's eyes shot open searching for signs he was teasing, finding none.

"I'll be right back." Hunter offered a small smile, kissed Jesse's forehead and was off to the kitchen with Maggie hot on his heels. Jesse sighed running a hand down his face. He hadn't realized how much Hunter had grown, had changed since he left all those months ago. He had just talked Jesse down effectively and patiently without losing it himself, and admitted how it was affecting him. Jesse hadn't even once asked what had gone on in the time Hunter was back in New York, too preoccupied with his own self-pity. He took a cleansing breath and vowed to change that. Jesse stretched out, cracking his back and resituated himself in the corner of the couch with a painful groan. He leaned against the arm of the couch, casted leg stretched across the length of the couch, opposite leg propped on the floor.

"I can hear you thinking from way over here." Hunter smiled peering out from the kitchen.

"Can you come here a minute?" Jesse asked, wincing as he shifted to sit more upright.

"Mmhmm, dinner's in the oven, wine is chilling, and I may have found a calzone in the freezer that I think is six months old but I don't care, we definitely deserve it tonight." Hunter shimmied his shoulders a bit as he approached Jesse.

"C'mere." Jesse reached out gripping Hunter's wrist when he stepped close enough. He tugged gently, pulling Hunter down so he was seated on the couch between Jesse's thighs, Hunter's long legs draped over the leg Jesse had propped on the floor. Hunter landed with a quiet "*oof*" and slid his arm around Jesse's neck.

"Hi honey." Hunter bit back a smile. Jesse leaned his forehead on Hunter's shoulder.

"Tell me how therapy's going." Jesse murmured.

"We don't have to..." Hunter waved his hand dismissively.

"No I...would like to hear about it. Humor me?" He whispered, keeping his head down.

"Mmkay." Hunter toyed with the curls at the base of Jesse's neck, knowing it soothed him. "Embarrassingly enough, I like it. I'm enjoying it." He huffed out a laugh, "My therapist is from New York originally, so it's been kinda cathartic to discuss the plunders of the big city." Jesse hummed in acknowledgment. "I'm learning about myself, does that make sense?" Hunter scratched lightly on Jesse's scalp.

"Course it does. I see a difference in you." Jesse gave a quiet moan leaning into the touch.

"I feel different." Hunter smiled.

"Hunter..." Jesse breathed

"Mmhmm." Hunter hummed lacing the fingers of his free hand with Jesse's on his own lap.

"You don't have to tell me but, what happened in New York?"

"What made you ask that now?" Jesse pulled his head up to meet his eyes.

"I realize I haven't been very supportive of you. You've worked so hard on yourself. You've been here for me through this whole mess and before that you were willing to put your heart on the line and wait around for me to be ready to accept or reject you. I never asked how you were and I want you to know I care." Hunter smiled kissing Jesse gently.

"Okay, so New York was ten steps backwards. I was very hyper-aware of how lonely I was and sunk myself into work.

I soared back to success, artists were seeking me out from across the globe, but old habits die hard, so there were other things I used to cope." Hunter scrunched his eyebrows. "I was high when I got here, when I first came to see you. It was a rough detox, but it was the first time I detoxed surrounded by people who care. My parents, my sister, Shay, they were there for me. It gave me the headspace to evaluate myself and what I want, so I knew when you called me that I would be ready for whatever you had to say, that I loved you enough to let you go if that's what you chose." Hunter kept his composure, confident enough in their relationship that he would be supported in what he was admitting. Jesse, on the other hand, felt his chest tighten as Hunter spoke, dropping his head back to Hunter's shoulder to hide his emotion.

"I'm so sorry." Jesse whispered, breath hitching.

"You have nothing to apologize for. I walked away, you had the right to choose, though I can't say I'm not glad you chose me." Hunter hooked a finger under Jesse's chin, lifted his head and connected their lips. They kissed slowly, Hunter tilting Jesse's head to just the right angle, until the oven timer dinged. Hunter pulled him into a tight hug and pressed a kiss to his temple before going to serve their dinner. He returned with two plates of piping hot food and made a second trip for wine glasses before sitting back on the couch next to Jesse's knee, giving him enough space to eat.

"Your ribs feeling okay?" Hunter asked handing Jesse a plate and fork.

"Still sore." Jesse shrugged poking at his food.

"You can take pain pills before bed." Hunter said and Jesse grunted in return.

"Hey," Hunter paused, waiting for Jesse to make eye contact before continuing, "I love you." Hunter smiled and Jesse sighed happily, raising his wine glass.

153

"I love you too." He responded, the click of their glasses ringing through the room before they peeled off their dinner.

Excited anticipation awoke Hunter before his alarm could. The soft bed and warm body that once felt so foreign had now become his everyday. Hunter usually loved being held, but had taken up the roll of the big spoon since Jesse's accident. So there he laid, arm draped over Jesse's side, just under his tender ribs, thumb snuck up the hem of Jesse's sleep shirt, rubbing circles into the soft skin of his belly, knees tucked under Jesse, behind heavy plaster. Maggie had nestled in the bend of Hunter's knees, her head resting on his ankle. Hunter pressed soft, feather light kisses across Jesse's shoulder, back, neck. Maybe the big spoon would be his permanent spot after all. Hunter sighed in contentment, Jesse's short hairs at the nape of his neck fluttering in his warm breath. The alarm went off and Jesse stirred, groaning softly as he squirmed in discomfort. Jesse shut the alarm and nuzzled his back against Hunter's chest squeezing the hand that was draped over his body. Hunter could feel Jesse's muscles tense as the comfort of sleep left his body.

"Morning beautiful." Hunter whispered ghosting his lips on the shell of Jesse's ear. He placed soft kisses on the back of Jesse's neck down to his shoulder, ridding him of some tension he was carrying.

"Why are you waking me up?" Jesse mumbled sleepily.

"I have a surprise for you, we have to get ready soon." Hunter couldn't keep the smile off his face.

"Soon." Jesse groaned turning himself over to face Hunter, taking a moment to steady his breath.

"You okay?" Hunter hesitated to touch him.

"Mmhmm want to see you." Jesse moved his foot between Hunter's own as he leaned in for a kiss. Hunter returned it with fervor while his hand found Jesse's hip, circling his hipbone with the pad of his thumb that slipped in the hem of his sleep pants. Jesse hummed as they pulled apart and tucked himself under Hunter's chin.

"Do we have to get up?" Jesse asked and Hunter chuckled in reply.

"You won't be disappointed, promise." Hunter placed a kiss in his hair. Hunter got himself ready first, giving Jesse breakfast in bed to keep him busy for the time being. When he was dressed, in a white long sleeve Henley, a thick cable knit cardigan over it with its oversized cherry wood buttons fastened and dark jeans, he took out Jesse's clothes. Hunter had taken a pair of Jesse's old worn jeans and cut them at the thigh of one leg so he could wear them as the weather cooled. Needing help to get dressed was undesirable for Jesse and it frustrated him to no end, but seeing how Hunter modified his jeans, he couldn't help but smile fondly. He paired the jeans with a black and white plaid button up, easier to help him put on without jostling his sore ribs. Hunter handed him a glass of water and two pills for pain that he knew would help before they arrived at the surprise. Though they would typically walk, Hunter piled Jesse into the back seat of Jesse's own car and drove them the short distance to the docks. Jesse questioned him incessantly during the short drive and while Hunter helped drag him out of the car.

"Okay first of all you definitely have enough strength in your good leg to help me a little and second please shut up!"

Hunter gave an exasperated groan as he pulled Jesse from the car, arms laced under Jesse's. He laughed freely in reply.

"I could help, but this is way more fun." He turned his head pecking a kiss on Hunter's jaw. Hunter sighed dropping him back into the seat.

"You're a monster you know that?" Hunter smirked and Jesse reached up, grabbed the back of Hunter's head and pulled him into a kiss.

"I've been told. Okay, let's do this." Jesse smirked and planted his foot on the floor of the car helping raise himself out of the seat as Hunter pulled. Once upright, he balanced on the side of the car until he was handed his crutches to situate himself. Hunter grabbed a basket from the trunk and kept pace with him as they approached the docks.

"Hunter this isn't fair, like teasing a dog with a stick of meat." Jesse huffed, whining in protest.

"Will you just trust me?" Hunter smiled placing a hand on the small of his back as they walked down the dock to meet Jesse's crew. He was greeted with big smiles and fishy smelling half hugs. After catching him up on the newest happenings at sea, Jesse turned to Hunter with a smile.

"Thank you, it was nice to be back with my crew."

"Oh honey, that's not your surprise." Hunter rubbed his back gently. Two of the crew members pulled a chair over and Hunter guided Jesse to sit, taking his crutches. The two men carried Jesse in the chair onto a pontoon. Hunter helped him maneuver himself from the chair to the bench, settled in next to him and snaked an arm around his waist as they departed the dock.

"Surprise." Hunter kissed Jesse's cheek, the smile on his face was proof of the success of his surprise. Jesse missed the water, bobbing with the waves, and the salty breeze in his curls. When the shoreline disappeared from sight, Hunter opened the basket and set up their lunch on the bench at the back of the pontoon. Warm, cheesy paninis filled with fried eggplant, roasted tomatoes, fresh basil, caramelized onions, and mozzarella drizzled with sweet, sticky balsamic glaze were their main course with thick cut fried potato wedges and dip on the side. Jesse's mouth watered before Hunter even finished unpacking their meal. They sat side by side, Jesse's leg propped up on the long cushioned bench seat they occupied, and enjoyed their sandwiches with satisfied hums.

"Can't wait to be back out here every day." Jesse mused as he bit into the crunchy bread.

"You're not nervous? Not apprehensive at all?" Hunter asked pulling at a stubborn string of cheese.

"Nah. I know how to handle myself out here. I'm confident in my sailing." Jesse nodded.

"Hmm." Hunter hummed noncommittally.

"What?"

"You...nothing." Hunter worried his lip thinking better of bringing it up.

Jesse sighed and pulled Hunter into his side, that spot that was made for him. "Listen, I know the ocean is powerful, I know that scares you and I get it, but I don't regret what I did." He stated, fingers trailing up and down Hunter's bicep. "It was a matter of seconds. Marshall went over, I'm not sure how. The crew tossed out life preservers, ring buoys, flotations but he was in shock, couldn't fight the current to get to what was there. I didn't even think, I just jumped. I told you, the crew comes home together, we all have someone to come back for and we are responsible for one another. I'm a strong swimmer, I knew I could make it back, so I got him, we both held on, but the current got the best of me." Hunter wrapped both arms tightly around Jesse's waist. "We were maybe a hundred yards out from the lighthouse. I got pulled under,

I felt my body hit the rocks, drag down against them, then I hit my head. Next thing I knew I woke up to your parents, feeling like I was run over by a truck. I don't know how they pulled me out," He shrugged, "but I'm grateful as hell."

"That sounds terrifying." Hunter shuttered squeezing rhythmically, repetitively on Jesse's thigh.

"I guess it was. I don't remember being afraid, I know that sounds crazy." Jesse huffed a laugh and rubbed soothing circles on Hunter's back. "I'm here now though and even with my lack of ability to do much of anything, I'm happy. My life feels like it's finally falling into place, thanks to you." Jesse smiled pressing a kiss to Hunter's head. He was seemingly on the verge of panic, but Jesse could see him working to fight against it. Jesse pulled him up and onto his thigh, wrapping his arms around Hunter's waist.

"I love you." Jesse breathed quietly.

"I love you too." Hunter whispered pressing their foreheads together, wrapping his arms around Jesse's neck.

Jesse smiled, "What will you do when I come back to work? When I get the all clear?"

"I do have a job Jesse." Hunter gave a lopsided smile, calming easily in Jesse's arms.

"Yeah, waiting tables Hunter. You left for New York for work, that's not something you should just settle for." Jesse dragged his calloused fingers along the small of Hunter's back where his sweater parted from his jeans, skin to skin. Hunter gave a full body shutter, warmth spreading through him from the comforting contact.

"The museum offered me an international buying position." He spoke softly, his head resting in the crook between Jesse's neck and shoulder. "I turned it down and they increased the offer. I told them I need time." He sighed, "I have an obligation to care for someone right now and to help my parents out at the restaurant. I told them I'll reach back out in January, see if the position is still available."

"You should take it." Jesse said. Hunter pulled back to look at him.

"I don't have the time right now. It's a big undertaking and I want to be available for you."

Jesse smiled brightly, "You are Hunter, but you have to take care of your wants too. I want that for you."

"I'll think about it okay?" Hunter tucked his smile into his cheek and Jesse nodded, "I have been thinking about this town."

"What about it?" Jesse tilted his head questioningly.

"That museum you took me to, the deGarthe gallery?" Hunter started and Jesse nodded smiling at the memory, "The space isn't being utilized how it could be. It's a beautiful space, inside and out. The grounds, the sculpture garden, would make a superlative event space." Hunter mused looking out at the horizon, his fingers playing with the curls he complained were growing too long on the back of Jesse's head. "I can picture it, catering from Catch of the Day, fresh flowers and greenery, maybe some cedar wood trellis."

"That sounds beautiful." Jesse smiled, "Bring it up at the next town hall. I guarantee they'll say yes." Jesse pressed a kiss to his jaw and resumed his lunch, keeping Hunter pressed to his side even after he slid from Jesse's lap. When their lunch scraps were cleaned up, Jesse leaned back with his arm around Hunter.

"Thank you, this was such a perfect day."

"I was hoping it would be enough to get you through the next few weeks." Hunter closed his eyes against the wind as the boat sped back to the docks.

"I have to accept it. I won't be back with my crew for months." Jesse sighed resigning to it. "I needed to be out here, to remember what happened, I think, to realize. I have no strength barely any mobility, I'll be more a burden than a help to my crew until my body is cooperating."

"I'm sorry honey." Hunter squeezed his hand.

"I'm not, not anymore. I'm going to enjoy the time I have with you and Maggie." Jesse smiled feeling somehow lighter as the boat docked.

A week later, Hunter came home from work to a waxed, grey oak desk, three drawers on the right side and a lift top for more storage. A cushioned navy chair in matching grey oak sat tucked underneath. Upon approaching, he found a note in Jesse's messy scrawl. *"Take the job!"* Hunter chuckled lightly shaking his head.

"Where are you hiding?" He called into the quiet house. Maggie bounded out of the bedroom at the sound of his voice, greeting him by standing on her hind legs and licking his face. He followed her back to the bedroom where Jesse was pulling himself off the bed to balance on crutches with a grunt. Hunter was on him in a flash, arms snaked around Jesse's waist, effectively knocking his crutches to the ground and crashing their mouths together, met with a surprised grunt from Jesse before he melted into Hunter's arms. Jesse braced himself on Hunter's shoulders as he pulled back, breathless.

"Hello to you too." Jesse breathed meeting his eyes, burning bright with desire.

"What are you trying to do to me?" Hunter purred latching onto Jesse's neck, beginning to mark his territory.

"Just…mmm getting you a nice present." Jesse tightened his grip on Hunter's shoulders, his stable leg going weak at the knee. Luckily Hunter had his waist in a vice grip, their hips and torsos flush against one another.

"You're never going to be able to get rid of me. Long office days, your incredible cooking filling the place with delectable smells, trying to distract me from my work with sneaky kisses. I'm going to want to stay forever." Hunter kissed him as he spoke, pausing his musings to show his appreciation.

Jesse moaned softly, tilting his head back, allowing Hunter access to the spot on the crook of his neck he loved so much. "Then stay with me baby."

"Always do." Hunter smirked gently dragging his teeth against the red mark he was creating on Jesse's neck.

"Mmm yeah, but I mean, move in with me." Jesse's breathing was growing heavy, heat burning in his chest. He had been wanting to ask, but was afraid Hunter would think he was being asked to be his caretaker. Jesse loved falling asleep to Hunter, waking up to him, their domestic routines and the way they were growing to know one another, but more than that, he wanted their lives tangled as one. He realized, when folding his laundry, stacking it neatly in the armoire, that he wanted Hunter's sweaters mixed in with his own, wanted them to share the space. Hunter froze, meeting Jesse's eyes, he wanted to be sure of the request. Jesse dragged the cool pad of his thumb against Hunter's swollen lower lip.

"I mean it. I want this to be ours, if you want that too?" Jesse raised the pitch of his voice to give an option. Hunter nodded dumbly, pressing a kiss to the thumb Jesse still rested on his lip.

"I, yes. Yes that would be…I would love that." Hunter smiled. Despite the effort, it had taken Jesse to get dressed and out of bed, he put up no argument when Hunter laid him back down and gently unraveled him.

Jesse loved the grounding weight of Hunter's boneless sweaty body on his, watching the jet black mop of hair rise and fall with his own still heaving breaths where Hunter was pillowed on Jesse's chest. Jesse traced his fingers over the cresting and falling muscles of Hunter's back, dewy to the touch.

"Jesse." Hunter murmured turning his head, cushioning his chin atop his hand on Jesse's sternum, looking up with a blissed out smile.

"Mmm?" Jesse smiled back, pushing back a tuft of hair that had escaped to Hunter's forehead.

Hunter felt his cheeks pull with a Cheshire cat-like grin as he proclaimed with confidence, "I'm home."

Epilogue

Hunter flipped through the pages on his clipboard checking off items on his list as he slowly paced the wharf. He took a deep calming breath and let it out, loud and slow, the scent of salt tickling his nose. He straightened his emerald green crew neck sweater accented with three panels of different textures across his shoulders, chest, and torso, the hems a cable knit to contrast the other patterns. It had been sent to him as a gift from a prospective museum client in Ireland who insisted he needed to add the merino wool sweater to his wardrobe. With the oatmeal thermal underneath, the sweater kept him comfortably warm in the early winter of Peggy's Cove. He knew it would be perfect for opening day of the Festival of Holidays the moment he opened it, and paired with chocolate brown jeans and boots it completed his holiday themed look. Hunter had been working in international buying for nearly three months with two new museum exhibits to prove it. He was thrilled with the position and even more thrilled that he could do it from the comfort of his home in the Cove. Hunter had developed his time management skills through his new line of work, still making himself available to wait tables at the restaurant and be at Jesse's disposal during his lengthy recovery. Hunter and Jesse had partnered together to plan the Festival of Holidays, a celebration that was projected to outdo the earnings of last year's festival by double. Hunter looked up from his lists to glance at his watch and then the docks. Jesse had been due back a half hour ago. Hunter's mom had taken him to physical therapy, since he was otherwise occupied with the setup, and to pick up the final paperwork signing the care of the deGarthe property over to them. After an in depth proposal to the counsel, they were approved to clean up the deGarthe gallery and grounds and begin hosting events in the space. Hunter placed his clipboard on one of the wooden booths that had been put together and shook out his hands rapidly, huffing out a breath to push away the creeping anxiety. Jesse was never late and everything on his lists had gone exactly according to plan, he was waiting for the one thing that would trip up the day.

"Hey! You good?" Katie said as she and Shay joined him, sliding her arm around his shoulders.

"Mmhmm yeah. You haven't seen Jesse right? Or mom?" He asked and Katie shook her head.

"No sorry. They'll be back soon I'm sure!"

"Here take the edge off." Shay smiled handing Hunter a glass of bubbly red liquid with floating cranberries and a cinnamon stick poking out of the top. "Christmas punch, from Nancy at the Maplewood Distillery." The three clicked their matching glasses together.

"Whoa, that's good!" Hunter smiled wrapping his arms around Katie in a hug.

"Mmhmm, everything looks fantastic! Why don't you let us take the final sweep." Shay said taking his board off of the table.

"You don't have to. Go enjoy yourselves."

"You enjoy! Sit back and take it in before the rush, we've got this." Katie smiled kissing his cheek and bounded off with Shay, leaving him to sip down his cocktail. Hunter watched the blue sky turn gold as the sun began its descent and his cup became empty. He closed his eyes against the cold ocean breeze and steeled himself to open the gates and begin the festival. Before he could turn, strong arms snuck around his waist and warm lips pressed on his neck. Hunter sighed, tension slowly leaving his body muscle by muscle, he need not open his eyes to know he was safe.

"There you are." Hunter whispered spinning in Jesse's arms to kiss him properly, his long arms wrapped tightly around Jesse's neck. Jesse's red cashmere sweater complimented Hunter's deep green. Hunter purchased him his first cashmere with his earnings from the new job and insisted he wear it for the festival with black jeans. Jesse had graduated from the hard cast to a boot and a brace that kept his knee stabilized.

"What'd you miss me or something?" Jesse asked biting Hunter's lip gently, his thumbs sneaking up the hem of Hunter's layers to settle in his back dimples. Hunter let out a breath he was unaware he had been holding, the skin-to-skin touch comforting him.

"You were scheduled to be here an hour ago. When I'm done with you my mother will receive the same lecture on communicating delays so I can keep my sanity and not imagine my boyfriend and mother at the bottom of an ocean somewhere." Hunter rushed out the words seemingly in one breath, a slight buzz lingering from his cocktail.

"You know physical therapy is inland, we weren't on a boat." Jesse smirked with a teasing lilt to his voice and Hunter pouted at him, "I know I know, I'm sorry." Jesse kissed him soundly and slid his arms off Hunter's waist, taking his hand. "Come for a walk with me."

"The festival's about to start, I have to go count the guests and check in on vendors." Hunter gesticulated with his free hand.

"I think they can manage without you for a minute. Come on." Jesse kissed his knuckles and dragged him away from the wharf, the buzz of the growing crowd dissipating as they walked. Jesse's stilted gait was a result of the height of the boot and stiffness of the knee brace. He leaned lightly against Hunter to alleviate some of the pain in his hip as they walked.

"Where are we going?" Hunter asked, peering over his shoulder at the shrinking holiday lights.

"Trust me." Jesse smiled, something flickering in his eyes that Hunter couldn't put his finger on.

"Mmkay." Hunter smiled squeezing his hand. Jesse led him to the one story distressed white house with blue shutters. The weathered Art Gallery sign coming into view. Hunter pulled his lips between his teeth to hide his growing smile. Jesse unhinged the white picket fence gate, letting them onto the property and took the path leading to the sculpture garden.

"This is ours now. I bet you can't wait to see your vision come to life." Jesse spoke softly, his voice rough, shaky.

"My vision?" Hunter questioned as they walked down the cobblestone path to the garden. A soft glow filled the garden, illuminated by strings of fairy lights weaved in cedar wood trellises. Hunter's eyes scanned the decorated garden until they fell on a patch of cream and maroon colored magnolias. His breath hitched in his chest.

"My vision." Hunter breathed almost silently.

"I may have snooped through your sketch book and gotten a jump start." Jesse smiled, biting his lip in anticipation. "I don't know what to say." Hunter wandered away from him, gently unlacing their fingers to take a closer look. After closely analyzing the setup, a grin plastered on his face, dimples out, tears pooling in the corners of his eyes, he took a shaky breath. "Jesse this is incredible, exactly as I pictured it, but better in person." He spun to face Jesse and let out a gasp of surprise and a choked *"oh my gosh"*, tears spilling over against his own will. Jesse had taken the opportunity to lower himself gingerly to one knee, black velvet box popped open in his hands.

"Hunter Davis, from the moment I met you I knew you were someone special. You continue to grow and change becoming a more authentic version of yourself every day. You make me want to be my best self, you dragged me through one of the lowest points of my life. You gave me the family I have always wanted. When you walked in my door with a bouquet of flowers for me, that's when I knew I wanted to marry you." Jesse's voice cracked as he spoke, overcome with emotion. Hunter stood a few feet in front of him, holding his breath to keep quiet enough to hear what Jesse had to say. "So now I finally get to ask you, Hunter will you marry me?" Jesse smiled, his own eyes damp as Hunter launched himself to his knees and into Jesse's arms.

"Yes, yes!" Hunter buried his face in Jesse's neck, met with giddy laughter as Jesse let go of his nerves and held Hunter close.

"I love you baby." Jesse kissed his temple and Hunter pulled back, staring into Jesse's warm, whiskey eyes. He knew he would be forever at home in those earnest eyes.

"I love you Jesse." Hunter kissed him soundly, lovingly. They stood from the ground, Hunter helping Jesse to his feet and Jesse slipped the ring on his finger. Hunter admired it with a smile, white gold band with a matte finish, featuring twenty round black diamonds in a brushed channel setting around the middle. They rejoined the festival as fiancés and announced the happy news to their family and friends with a town wide toast celebrating their future union and the town that they had both once tried desperately to escape, that had brought them both a happiness they never knew they could have; the town that became their home.

About the Author

Michelle Cuce is a Disney princess at heart, a dreamer, a wisher, a teacher, a lover of happily ever afters, and now...an author! Her roots are in her New York home with her AMAZING family, including her mother, father, given sister/chosen best friend and her dog, Reeses Pieces. Michelle is always up for an adventure, but also loves to cuddle up with a cup of tea and a good book. She is ready to travel at the drop of a hat and adores all things Disney. Michelle draws inspiration from all of her life's journeys as well as the stories of those she meets. Join her on her new endeavor, which took off during the dark days of the pandemic, when everything was unknown and the only sure thing was writing. Something that acted as her own escape from reality will take you into a world of hardships, family, friends and new love.